Sea Dar

In my dream the hands were reaching
down, down into the dark; that's what I always felt.

Willie Cormack hates the sea. He sees it in his nightmares, the raging ocean full of the ghosts of drowned fishermen, beckoning to him. But Willie lives on a peninsula on the west coast of Ireland and the sea is all around him. The only way to make a living is from the sea, and Willie is afraid of his future.

And then a lone sailor is shipwrecked on the coast in a storm and the tiny community is thrown into turmoil by the stranger who is so suddenly thrust among them. In the atmosphere of bigotry and suspicion that follows, a terrible tragedy seems inevitable unless Willie can meet his own fears face to face and pit himself against the very elements that haunt his dreams.

GATTI has always enjoyed making up stories, and reading them. daydreamed his time away at school, he gained a BA(Hons.) in English at Oxford University and then had various jobs, including being a warehouseman, a van driver, a children's book editor, and an EFL teacher, before becoming an English teacher. He is now head of English at a girl's school in Surrey. He taught for a while at a school in Dublin and lived on the west coast of Ireland for a couple of years, which is where he returns every summer, and where he has set *Sea Dance*, his first novel for Oxford University Press.

Sea Dance

Sea Dance

Will Gatti

OXFORD
UNIVERSITY PRESS

Oxford University Press, Great Clarendon Street, Oxford OX2 6DP

Oxford New York

Athens Auckland Bangkok Bogotá Buenos Aires
Calcutta Cape Town Chennai Dar es Salaam
Delhi Florence Hong Kong Istanbul Karachi
Kuala Lumpur Madrid Melbourne Mexico City
Mumbai Nairobi Paris São Paulo Singapore
Taipei Tokyo Toronto Warsaw

and associated companies in
Berlin Ibadan

Oxford is a trade mark of Oxford University Press

British Library Cataloguing in Publication Data
Data available

Cover illustration by Sam Hadley

ISBN 0 19 271803 7

Printed and bound in Great Britain by
Biddles Ltd, Guildford and King's Lynn

To friends in the West

Author's Note

Although all the characters in the story are fictional, two events I refer to did take place, though not in the way I have described them. The first is the tragic accident that took place off the Inishkea Islands on 28 October 1927 when a wild and sudden storm scattered a fleet of curraghs out night fishing. Ten men were drowned. Only two fishermen survived—John and Anthony Meenaghan. They had almost made it back to the safety of the island when a savage gust sped them back into the high seas. Yet somehow they kept themselves afloat and were eventually cast up on the mainland.

The second incident is that of the yacht driven aground in Elly Bay, but of this I know little; only that the sailor was alone, was from North Africa, that he was cared for on the Mullet and eventually helped to return home. Even a few years back the hull of the wrecked boat was visible at the edge of the bay.

The two stories haunted me and somehow became intertwined.

One

I sometimes wonder whether anyone would believe the luck of it, you know, were I to let on. And when I say luck, I don't mean the good sort; the sort that would have Anna Macbraid falling in love with you because you were there playing the fiddle so sweetly at the dance that she would just faint into your arms.

Dream on!

When I say luck, I mean the bad black sort. I mean a curse. I'll tell you what it is, though maybe it won't mean much to you.

Where I live is called the Mullet, nothing but a long lick of land, sandy land at that, sticking out into the ocean. It's a peninsula, so Mrs Sweeney told me in her geography class when I was seven years old and not minding what she was saying till she hit me on the back of me legs with her strap Then it surely stuck in me head and I've never forgotten it from then till this day now. Not that it's a word I use, because it makes me think of cooking, don't ask me why, and the whole point of what I'm telling you is that it is sea that surrounds me.

To the east there is Blacksod Bay five miles across, south there is the wide mouth of the bay with nothing but the green sloping hump of Duvillaun Island till you get to the cliffs of Achill Island, which is hardly an island at all on account you can drive across to it. And then west there are the Inishkea Islands where my family are from; and then there is nothing but the whole of the wide, broad Atlantic which spends nine months of the year battering in at us.

And so what is this bad luck?

My bad luck is the sea. It is all around me. It is in my family, for they were all islanders and fishermen at one time, and it is in my friends. And time was, when I was a small lad, I could barely walk the strand without getting a cold sweat down my spine. It's true, my friends might be playing or picking cockles but put me within spitting distance of the water and I'd be no good at all. And I dream of the sea endlessly, tossing and moaning like a sick baby. Thank God I don't share a room any more. When I was small, my brothers would kill me for yelling out in my sleep and waking them, beating me with a pillow till I learned to keep quiet. But they are gone now and I am not sad about that at all.

I am fourteen now and I've taught myself not to make any kind of fuss, for what's the point in that. Don't get me wrong, it doesn't kill me seeing the water out there, flat and blue on a rare fine summer's day, or even wild and grey, frothing at the shoreline. I can watch it, for hours sometimes, and I do, training myself not to mind it.

I used to think I'd have to leave this place when I was grown, that I would go somewhere deep inland where the only water would be what comes out of a tap. And then I would have my mother writing and writing to me and telling me that I am breaking her heart for leaving, but not to worry for she would never stand in the way of her sons even though they were bent on making her life a misery. My mother has a way of putting things, you know, that makes it hard to argue with her, or that's what I find.

My leaving might bother my father a wee bit too, not that he lets on much about his feelings. He likes to talk on about the islands, and how it was in them days out there; and lucky for him I do like to listen, and I'm the only one in the family that does. Maybe that is why it never bothered him when my two brothers upped and left home. Neither of them had time for my father.

One time I talked about my fear of the sea with Ian—he's my best friend—but he said I was cracked which was no great comfort. There was no one else I could tell, only our priest Father Paul, but, to be honest with you, and it's probably a sin to admit it, I don't like him, and I certainly don't trust him. He rides horses! Who ever heard of a regular priest riding a horse?

The odd thing is I like it here and have no yearning to be anywhere else. Sometimes I think it's like the edge of the world; one giant step west and you could topple into space. I have a lot of time for those fellas who thought the world was flat, and sure I would never have set sail with Brendan, despite him being a saint and living on another island only a little way up the coast, Inishglora.

We, that is my family and Ian, and his Auntie Brede and about twenty other households in all, live on the south-western tip of the Mullet, in the village of Glosh. Not that it's really much of a village, more a scattering of houses on the side of Termon Hill, looking out to Inishkea North and Inishkea South. And every single household in Glosh owns land on those two islands, for we are all island folk, even those of us, like me, who were born on the mainland.

There is something different about island people that marks them out from others; it's hard to explain, but you can just tell: a way of walking, a way of greeting . . . perhaps we'll lose it in time for I can't see any of us going back out there to live again. And yet it wasn't so long ago that the islands were full of life.

My father was born on the south island and lived there until he was my age now. But in 1932 they were all brought over to the Mullet; the heart had gone out of them since the terrible storm of 1927, but I don't like to think of that too much.

God knows, though, I sometimes believe I think too much, thoughts drifting in and out of my head like the gulls that are forever floating along the shoreline. Ah well, that's me, William John Cormack, dreamer, and that is exactly what I was doing on that day of the dance, the day life changed here for ever.

I was sitting up on the hill above our house and I could see a storm building right out there on the ocean. Even with the sun warm on my face I could tell it was coming. It maybe wouldn't reach us for a while but it would come surely enough. It's not hard to read the weather living where we do. All you have to do is look west and there it is: pure blue or heavy banks of cloud of one sort or another.

That day there was a line of black cloud right down low on the horizon and a kind of yellow in the sky above it, and the air thicker than it should have been. And yet there are times when a storm will come out of nowhere, waves suddenly cracking up to the size of mountains, green and hungry for anything in their way. But the one coming wasn't like that, no sailor worth his salt would be caught half asleep by it; sure I could see it maybe four hours away and what did I know about sailing the seas.

I think it was then I had the first whispering of a tune forming in me head. I tried to catch it but I couldn't find the right notes and I was part sleepy anyway. So, I stretched out my legs and leaned my head back against the wall of the signal tower that stands halfway up Termon Hill, no more than a couple of hundred yards above my own house, and a good long way from any wave, you can be sure of that.

I always go there whenever I need a bit of space and quiet to practise the fiddle or work on a tune. I don't know where I have the music from. Brede says neither my father nor my mother ever sang a note. I would like to think it is how I'll earn myself a living when I leave school or college, but the only musicians I know around here are either that old you

4

wouldn't want to be like them or given over to the drink, and that's surely a waste.

I think the tower was built in the war, the Second World War, though it could have been the First, and I don't know who they ever wanted to signal to from there. There were a pair of ravens nesting here last summer but they went away. I keep coming up here hoping that they will be back.

I could have drifted off easy, half lying there as I was, if I hadn't heard Ian yelling at me. My eyes were closed and the sun was full on my face and the ground under my backside was as dry as a bone; school was over for the whole summer, and the couple of fields we have wouldn't be ready for cutting for at least another week, that's if we could get Mick Gowry and his combine to come when he said he would, which would be something in the line of a miracle.

My mother says it's unnatural me liking to go off on my own so much. My Da grunts but says nothing. I tell them I'm planning for the future, which has a small part of truth in it, I suppose. Mostly, though, I stare out towards the ocean and try to tell myself that it's no worse than a bath, only bigger, which doesn't really convince me.

And then I tend to think about Anna, 'lovely raven-haired Anna', which is what people like my mother call her. She's in the top class, three years older than me and Ian, but that doesn't stop us arguing about her. She's so gorgeous she'd make a saint spin.

'Willie!'

I didn't bother to lift me head, for it wouldn't stop him running nor yelling. Very little would ever stop Ian, apart from his auntie, that is.

'Willie, you lazy gobshite . . . ' And I've no doubt he would have said more but he was out of breath from running up the hill, and his red freckled face was half bursting with the sweat and heat.

5

I felt almost sorry for him but it's hardly decent to be pitying your friends and so I said, 'What is it, you little midget?' He is small but not so much as you might worry about him, just enough for him to be a touch sensitive about it; the only thing I reckon he is sensitive about.

I know and he's my best friend. But you have to mind a good friend at all times and stop him from becoming either swollen headed or generally impossible, that's what I think, and I'm sure that if Ian ever stopped to think, that would be close enough to his own opinion too.

'Jesus, I've a mind to let you rot here and not tell you,' he flopped down beside me, disgruntled, 'what I was going to tell you.'

'Is that right?' It is a fact that I have the knack of irritating the hell out of people. I don't know where I get it, none of my family are half as irritating as me, well not in the same way anyhow. It is just that it's so obvious sometimes how people want you to behave or what they want you to say, and I suppose there is something in me that makes me then want to do the opposite. It doesn't make me a favourite at school and it always rattles Ian, though of course he pretends he doesn't notice.

'Aye, it is.' He plucked a piece of grass, stuck it between his teeth and began to whistle. I don't know where he gets it from but he can whistle sweet as a bird. All sailors can whistle, he says.

The two of us have agreed that if we get the exams we'll go up to college in Donegal together, but he'll end up fishing, I reckon, whatever we study. He has to be on the sea in exact direct proportion to me being on the land. We're a fairly odd pair, wouldn't you say?

I was happy enough dreaming on, but himself has the patience of a wasp. 'Well?' says he.

'Well what?'

'Don't you want to know?' He tossed away the stem of

grass. 'I don't know why I bother with you at all. You're so lazy, you'd never do anything. You'd never be the one to organize us getting into the dance, would you?'

Now this did interest me. There was to be a big dance at Barratt's Bar in Aghleam that night and there was a band playing: Jinny Jinx. Everybody was saying how good they were because they were from Galway and they were meant to be like The Saw Doctors, probably because they're from Galway too. Anyway it was an event. We don't get so many rock bands making it this far into Erris let alone down the long stretch of the Mullet to where we are.

The black bind of it was that we hadn't a penny, and to add to that, Ian's Auntie Brede was set against him stepping into a pub and starting bad ways, and mine weren't so happy about it either. They wouldn't stop me if I set my mind on it, but they wouldn't give me the five pounds which is what the door money was to be. I gave him a yawn.

'Anyone with a couple of quid in their pockets could organize us getting into the dance.'

'Oh yes, and when did you have money?'

I wasn't going to dignify that with a reply.

He snorted. 'See! Well, what would you say if I told you that not only could we go to the dance free but that we could earn a few bob while we were there and all.'

'You did not!'

He looked smug.

'You did? You've a brain after all. That's a miracle . . . But what about Brede . . . ?'

'Don't be daft. I'm not a babby.'

That would be news to his auntie but it wasn't for me to comment so I sat up and dusted my hands against my jeans. 'How much?'

He knew I was impressed and was grinning so wide his mouth looked set to crack his head in half. 'How much what?'

'How much money?'

'A fiver. A fiver a piece for setting out the place, and more if we'll stay to do the bottles and washing and that. Jerry is off sick and there's no one else to help and you know how I got it, do you? Anna fixed it up for us, how about that?'

Anna! He'd be impossible for a week but you had to give credit to the man. 'She'd never look at you.'

'She promised me a dance and all.'

I hit him.

Ian was the one who saw the boat first. We were down at the road, ready to cut along the lane where we live, him and Brede on one side and me and my family on the other. She was way out, coming up from the south, clearing Achill Head by a long mile, and the sky purple black behind it.

'She'll be lucky to escape that,' he said, his hand shading his eye from the full sun that we were standing in.

There was something in his voice that made me stop and look again. I could just make her out, pure white and running free ahead of the black storm, like a bird, a tern maybe, so tiny against that mountain of cloud. Jeez, I would not have liked to have been one of her crew, I can tell you that.

'She'll be all right,' I said, 'won't she?'

'Don't know. Too far off to tell.' He pulled a face. 'She's bound to have a radio, anyhow, so she'll call if she needs help.' And then, as I bent to pick up my fiddle case, he said, 'Maybe I'll phone Francis when we get to Aghleam.'

'Sure. Good idea,' I said.

Francis would probably know anyway. There's not a lot that he misses. He's the keeper of the lights at Blacksod, the little harbour just the other side of the hill from us, and he has a fishing boat. Ian goes out with him sometimes on his boat, and is friendly with his son. I don't know him so well on account of my two feet having to be stuck so firmly on the land.

Anyway, I told myself, we have a powerful lifeboat at Ballyglass at the north-eastern end of the Mullet. But it is still a lonely stretch of coast here, and a man who gets in trouble needs a fair slice of luck to find safe haven.

It's a mad thing that none of us at Glosh have the telephone yet. I sometimes think the old islanders still want to be cut off, as much as they can. Though if you ask any one of them, they'll all say the same thing: that they don't want the phone because of the expense.

My mother has said that perhaps it would be nice, and the boys would be able to ring her up once in a while. My father snorts when she says things like that.

'Them phone us? Them bearing the expense! More like you'll be ringing Chicago, and I'll be paying the bill. And sure where will I have the few pounds for a pint then?'

Meanwhile there's the pay phone in the village if we have an emergency, and that's only a short bicycle ride away.

Anyway, once Ian said he'd phone, we both put that wee boat and her crew out of our minds. It was the dance we were thinking of mainly.

Home was a mistake.

Patrick—he's the baby of the family, four years old and the sisters spoil him—was sick, face red as a tomato and bawling; Dad was at the back door, putting on his cap, escaping; he always did when things got rocky. Jeanie was behind Mum, looking smug. She's twelve, the second youngest. We get on all right but she and her friends can sometimes get annoying at school, calling me 'dreaming Willie' which is a stupid thing to call anyone, and following me and Ian around when they should be off skipping and doing girl things.

There was no sign of Mary, she's the eldest now that the boys have left. I like Mary a lot. She doesn't go shouting and yelling. I think she's more like Dad than Mum.

'Where the divil have you been?' My mother is not a tall woman, nor fat neither, but all the same is sort of forceful, if you know what I mean, and she has a knack of doing more than one thing at a time which is enough to make you go a wee bit dizzy. There she was boiling up something horrid to swab Patrick with, hands doing figures of eight over the stove, and all the time she was looking over at me, trying to grip me with her angry eyes. When she does that I make a point of looking over her head.

'Why do you want to know?' I asked, and it seemed a reasonable enough question to me.

'Don't you talk to me like that!'

Neither cool nor calm ever works in our house. 'Like what?' I said. God knows, I sometimes think that what I say goes through a special mixing machine because she can hear things in what I've said that I swear I never dreamed of.

'You were to clear your room, because your brothers are home tonight. Or,' she said, sarcastically, 'had you forgotten? So busy dreaming up some scheme with that no-good Ian Carey that you had no time for your own family, though you haven't seen them for two years. And you said you would run the messages for me because Patrick isn't well and . . . ' Up went young Patrick, tucked under one arm, his red face stuck wide with surprise, and in went whatever horrible mixture she'd been boiling.

She was right, of course. I had forgotten. Not about the brothers coming home. They were strangers to me now and I was quite curious to see what they were like, though the truth is I had never been close to them. Gary was all right, bit of a jack the lad, but OK, you know, easy going. John James was different. Dad always said he was ambitious, would go places. Well, he did, he went to America.

'. . . and I'm worked to the bone as it is . . .'

'Sorry . . .' Ah well, it was hardly the crime of the century.

'I suppose you were just lolling about. Mother of God, you never do anything to help anyone. Will you get on and clear your room.'

I sometimes think that if words were water she could drown acres.

'Sorry.'

She turned away, coddling the wee lad, all soft and petting now, and sure Patrick causes more grief in our house than the rest of us children put together. I don't mind at all.

I sidled past her, and disappeared to my room. It was certainly no time to be announcing that I was off to the dance to earn a bit of cash.

I piled all my stuff into the built-in cupboard, leaving the brothers the chest. I didn't bother setting up a mattress for myself, maybe I could skip down to Ian's and sleep there. I got on better with his Auntie Brede than he did himself, so that wouldn't be a problem. I changed into a clean pair of jeans and would have given myself a wash too, except I could hear the mighty Patrick yelling still, and Mum trying to shush him, so I took a chance and scrambled out of the window, and legged it up the lane.

I saw Dad at the crossroads where the lane meets the road to Aghleam. He was leaning back against a gate, having a smoke, looking back towards Achill in the south-west, and taking it easy, which was always his way.

'Bit warm at home?' he said.

'It was,' I said. 'Are you off for a drink?'

'Aye.' His eyes are blue, kind of shocking blue. They're the first thing you notice about him, though he's hitting sixty and more. I think he had a few girls running after him when he was a lad. Odd that, thinking about him being young. I wonder what happened that he settled for Mum?

'Did you see the boat?'

'Aye.' Of course he had. He has better sight than I have.

She'd moved a fair distance in the half hour I'd been down at the house, though she was still too far off for me to make out much detail: a single mast, two foresails by the look of it, which I'd have thought was risky with that storm on her tail, and the mainsail swung wide and fat with the wind. She must have been fair scudding along; but the sky was so dark behind her that I did wonder about her chances, and I knew he was wondering the same.

'What do you think?'

'I wouldn't like to be them.' He frowned and flicked away the butt of his fag as an old brown Ford pulled up beside us. My father was not a talkative man, but somehow he said an awful lot with very little. I found myself suddenly worried and yet what was that sailing boat to me? Not a thing, but I found myself imagining what those poor souls were feeling, with the wind and the sea beginning to whip at them, and the waves building up high, and the rain cracking in at them . . . 'Are you coming with me or waiting on Ian?'

'I'll wait.' I lifted my hand in greeting to the driver, Eamon Sweeney, my father's long-time drinking companion and one-time fishing partner. Eamon nodded and then they were gone. I cursed Ian for being slow, for it was likely that we would have to walk the couple of miles now, and the rain was almost on us.

He came jogging up the road about five minutes later and then we argued the whole way in; him complaining that I was stupid for not getting Eamon to wait. He's not always reasonable, Ian isn't.

The rain caught us just as we were coming into Aghleam, and we pelted the last hundred yards, and burst into

Barratt's wet and panting, and had to put up with Mickey Barratt battering on that we were late and it was hardly worth his while to pay such layabouts. He's like that. Always growling but wouldn't harm a soul unless they started trying to dismantle the place, which I can't ever remember happening, probably on account of Mickey having a reputation for considerable strength. I myself have seen him lift the tail of a car right up off the road for a joke one time. Right high up and let it drop with a mighty crash. I forgot who was inside but they had annoyed him, I think. I reckon they might have been strangers.

We, Ian and I, that is, were hard at work in the big bar; that's where the band were going to play. My father and Eamon and a few other men were in the snug. Most families would come later, for the music and the crack; and, sure, if you came this early you would only be spending more money. My father liked this time down here because all his pals would come in and they would have peace. Later it would be mayhem.

We had cleaned down the tables and moved them to the side, shifted the piano back against the wall—the band were meant to be great musicians so they would hardly want to play that out-of-tune old thing—swept the floor, and even lit a fire by the time the first of the younger regulars came bunching in and demanding pints. It was great. It was so busy Mickey had Ian and me pulling pints—and me, I had never done that before. My father saw me at it but said nothing. A couple of girls from our class, Ailish King and Jean Coyle, came over and started teasing us for being stuck behind the bar, but we paid them no mind.

Then the band rolled up and the music started and the place was hopping. Anna came in with a crowd and was dancing like a dervish. Ian was looking sick with worry, and he kept asking me if he should or if he shouldn't dance with her, he was that worried. But to give him his credit he

13

did ask her, and she smiled and whirled about, and he told me she gave him a kind of a hug at the end of it, but I didn't see that.

It was ten o'clock before you could blink. I'd seen my two brothers. They had arrived together and there had been terrific greeting and buying of rounds. They hadn't noticed me behind the bar until I said, 'How are you doing, John,' for I recognized him well enough though he was looking more like a Yank than an Irishman.

'Willie,' he said, 'you've grown. I would hardly have known you.' He smiled but I noticed he was half checking himself in the bar mirror at the same time.

'I recognized you.'

His face was smooth and tanned, his cuffs white, and his thick, curly, black hair slicked back and shiny off his forehead. He raised the full pint that I had drawn for him, and gave me a wink. 'We'll catch up later, boyo,' he said. 'All right?'

'Sure.'

And he moved back into the crowd. We didn't have a lot in common, John James and I. I saw him talking to Anna a bit later on.

Gary came up to me, and he was the same as ever, more than a quarter drunk, but smiling and friendly. We watched Anna and John James dancing, and he made some smart comment because they were dancing a bit slow, you know, and John James was holding her like he had a right, and Gary said, 'Always quick to score, our Johnnie.'

Neither of us had realized that Ian was standing right beside us, and he had been watching Anna too. And before I could stop him, he had scrambled over the bar, kicking a glass flying.

'Has he gone mad or what?' growled Mickey coming in from the snug.

I knew what was going to happen. 'Ian!' I yelled, but of course he couldn't hear me, so I scrabbled after him. I'm no midget but I swear everyone in that bar seemed nine foot tall, and I could hardly budge between them, and I was getting frantic. Then Gary was beside me, and somehow, I suppose long years spent in the pub, he had the right word, and the easy manner, and the sea divided for us: and then there we were on the dance floor.

It was a pantomime. The band were playing: the lead singer had his eye on the action. Anna was yelling, her face screwed up and angry, and then there was poor old Ian up on tiptoe, and John James's thick hand round his throat, and John James's smooth chin stuck out towards him, and whatever he was saying was not at all friendly. I saw his other hand tighten into a fist.

I grabbed Gary's arm. 'Do something,' I shouted. 'Stop him!'

Two

The manic jig the band had been belting through crashed to a stop and though you'd hardly call it silence, it was quiet enough to hear Ian cursing, looking my brother square in the eye, just waiting for him to batter him. I told you he was mad. I saw Anna turn her back on the two of them and force her way back towards the bar. I gave Gary a shove.

'Ah, mind me pint, Willie.'

'Do something!'

'It's only a scrap.'

Scrap, me eye. John James was big and whatever he'd been doing out in Chicago he'd lost none of the muscle he'd built up playing the football. He had Ian up on his toes, just with the one hand holding him tight round the neck.

The whole thing only took seconds, and most people were hardly aware of anything. The band kicked into a new number, the lead singer, a splinter of a fella in a scraggy sweatshirt and a scarf round his head like a pirate, jumping up and down like he wanted to hammer his head on the ceiling.

I shoved Gary out of my way, and grabbed Ian just as John James hit him, a short stab smack in the eye. I think he was going to hit him again, but Mick put him off: 'All right, that'll do now, John.'

For such a big man Mick Barratt could move through a crowd awful easy, maybe it was the size that did it, or his reputation. Anyway there he was, and it was all over, apart from the shame of being hustled out of there by Mick himself who was none too sympathetic to either of us.

'You're lucky I don't give you a battering on the other side of your face, Ian Carey. Jasus, you need some sense knocking into you. Take him home, Willie.' Then he pulled open the door and shoved us out.

I'd been hardly aware of the storm all the time we were inside. You couldn't hear it for the band and you couldn't feel it for the warmth of all that crowd laced with drink. But out here on the porch it was a howling black banshee of a night. I stuck my hand out of the shelter of the porch and the rain practically drilled holes through the skin.

'What do you say we wait here for it to ease? At least we'll keep dry and hear something of the music.'

Ian didn't answer, not a word of thanks for butting in and risking my neck over him. Just shoved his hands into his pockets, ducked his head, and walked out into the teeth of that gale.

'Where are you going?' I yelled. 'Where are you going, you blind eejit?' He didn't hear, so I had no choice but to light out after him, which I did, catching him just where the road rolls out of the village and off along the edge of the sea towards the quay at Blacksod.

Looking at the waves there, I wondered what a hurricane was like; sure we couldn't have been far off one. Jayz, they were towering so high I reckoned they would have smacked the gut out of anybody fool enough to walk out into them. All the beach was gone under the white froth and black water. Right up to the road the sea came, right where Ian and I stood. And we were on the sheltered side of the Mullet. God help any poor soul out in the deep water, that's what was going through my mind, and a sick queer feeling in my stomach which I get when the sea fear takes me.

I gripped Ian's arm. 'Let's go back, Ian! Come on . . . '

I had forgotten the yacht we'd seen earlier, two or three hours back, but when he pointed, and I squinted against the rain and spray to see what he was looking at, I remembered. And then I saw her light, the port light, green.

17

Close she seemed, there and then gone, the flash and then black. Nothing else.

'Did you manage to catch Francis?' I had to pull him towards me and shout in his ear to make myself heard.

'Aye.'

I could tell he had forgotten the brawl and the smack, he was that intent on trying to follow every heave and shudder of the yacht's frame. His face was pale and strained, the left eye half closed. He'd have a good mark tomorrow. 'She's awful close,' he shouted. 'Too close.'

My thoughts exactly.

It was weird seeing just one light and having to fill in the picture of the boat that went with that light. How tall a mast, how long—

And then there was a sudden tearing light in that darkness, a jagged rip of moonlight through the cloud, and for a moment we saw her clear. Her port hull was down in the water and she was wallowing sluggish with each wave that hit her. There was only a scrap of a jib up, but maybe anything more would have pulled her right over, I wouldn't know.

I expected to see crew, at least three on a boat her size for she was a good fifty foot long, but there was only one figure hunkered down behind the wheel in the cockpit, a small black shape. And then, as the flare died, the night closed in and they, the figure and the boat, were gone, save for her port light, winking crazily at us.

'She's heading for Elly Bay,' yelled Ian. Elly is the largest bay on the inshore side of the Mullet Peninsula. It's sandy, sheltered, and safe with a long gentle strand at low tide. Those daft enough to want to immerse themselves in the sea for pleasure, like tourists, walk for miles to get out of their depth. I've seen them at it.

'Will she make it?'

'She might.' He didn't sound convinced. Then it was his

18

turn to pull me. 'Come on, we have to get some of the men to help.'

The only help was back at Mick Barratt's pub. I made him wait while I went in. I didn't want another fight on my hands.

I forced my way through to the bar and gave the word to Mick. He pointed out Francis to me, and said he would get a couple of lads and follow on, if I thought my dad would take over behind the bar for him.

'Is he standing or sitting?' I asked.

'Standing,' said he.

'Then he'll manage.'

Francis was in a corner with his young wife and a couple of men from Blacksod, Richard Leary and a cousin of his called Jack. He could tell, as I made my way towards him, that it was serious and was up on his feet, his hand already reaching for his coat as I told him what I'd seen. He's sharp, Francis, not a man ever to waste time.

'A long line, life jackets and the rubber dinghy from the sailing school on the north side of the bay.' He turned to his wife, Pat, 'Phone them up at the school and have them get the dinghy ready to launch in five minutes. Willie, you come with me.'

The two men came with us, and Ian. We piled into the car. Mick and a crowd were running out of the pub as we drove off. I wondered how many of them would be in a fit state to do anything useful.

Francis drove slowly; sure, you couldn't go fast in that storm, not without risk of missing the road. All the time Francis was looking off to his right. 'There she is,' he said after we had been driving a short while. I could see nothing. 'And she's too close to the point. I must have given him the bearings half a dozen times . . . '

'So you did talk with him?'

19

'Aye, but I couldn't get much sense out of the man. He'd not even the right chart for this bit of coast.' He swung the car off the road and up to a looming ramshackle building, an old warehouse it had been and was now part of the school. 'I gave him bearings to bring him into the bay and up to Elly. Sure that's the only hope for him.'

'Is he alone?' asked Ian. 'We only saw the one man at the wheel.'

'Didn't say. He sounded foreign as bejasus.'

He pulled on the handbrake and we all piled out and then gathered round the boot of the car from which he dug out a coil of light rope. I saw the lights of the second car further down the road making towards us.

'Was he Chinese?' I asked. That was about as foreign as I could think of.

'Excitable,' he said.

Who wouldn't be in a storm like that.

It was wild as a nightmare. Hunched backs, faces streaming with wet and every word shouted, then whipped away in the wind. We gathered in the lee of the building. Liam and Sean Keane, team leaders from the adventure school, tough lads, were all togged up in orange; the rest of us, including men from the second car, were just as we were, half drowned already. All of us waiting, eyes stretched into the darkness trying to pick out her lights.

If she managed to pass the point, and still had steerage, she could cut in and find shelter; not much though, for the wind had shifted round a little more to the south; but if the skipper misjudged it, or had troubles, he'd be driven straight on to the next set of rocks.

'All right now.' Francis gathered us round him, like we were a football team or something. 'First thing is: can we launch the dinghy—Liam?'

'Maybe. Got a good engine on her. Sean in the bow might stop her from flipping.'

'OK.'

'If they trailed the lifeline,' Mick suggested, 'we could haul them in once they reached your man.'

'No, it'll snag them,' said Francis. 'If they can, they have to lift the crew from the yacht; if not, the poor divils will just have to jump and with luck we'll haul them on board and then bring them back to the beach. We'll use the land line there and help to bring them in that way.'

I swear I was ready to do whatever I had to to help, but standing there in that spitting dark, with the waves hissing almost up to where we were, I seized up. I could feel my face set in the stupid grin that comes on me when I get like this. It means I'm only just on this side of screaming.

'Christ,' said Ian, 'you don't look so good.'

That was a comfort; I thought I probably looked insane. I could barely catch what Francis was saying, something about Mick being the shore man, anchoring the rest of us. I had no desire to be anchored, whatever it meant, but the others were all nodding, and that was it; we were moving.

The dinghy was brought out. Someone shouted, 'There she is!' and we saw her two lights, red and green, and then the moon broke free of cloud and we could pick her out, lurching like a drunk pig on her trotters, from crest to trough, and water breaking over her stern as if the whole ocean was set on drowning her.

Ian and I grabbed one side of the dinghy, Liam and Sean the other and we ran, straight down the slip, while the others made for the strand. There was no time for thinking now, and maybe that was just as well. Trying to time it as best we could between waves, we waded out into the water, Ian and Sean clinging to the bow while Liam hurled himself into the stern and started the engine, all in one go. The next wave caught the dinghy and wrenched her out of my hands, swinging her round, beam on to the sea.

There was nothing I could do. Nothing. I scrabbled back up the slip. Sure, one of those waves would suck you off to America. I caught my breath and tried to make out what was happening. I saw the dark hump of the dinghy poised like a plate on the tip of a wave, heard the howl of the motor lifted clean out of the water, and then a thump and roar. There was the white of the wake and they were gone, hitting the waves like fury, heading for the lights of the yacht . . . but where was Ian?

A wave caught me, and knocked me backwards up the slip and down on to me arse. I kept my head up. 'Ian!'

Then there he was, half swimming, half crawling on his hands and knees towards me, grinning. I told you he was mad. He was loving this, I reckon, about as much as I was hating it. 'The water's hardly cold at all,' he shouted.

I told you. Cracked.

We grabbed on to each other and then hurried as best we could along the shoreline till we reached the strand.

The boat was ghost white in the stormy moonlight. I saw her stern lifted high and then corkscrew round towards the shore but I couldn't see the helmsman, the skipper. Couldn't see him for the spray and the foam. Someone said the wind was easing, but I felt no change. Someone else said her keel must have struck sand for her to twist round like that, and that we ought to move before she broke her back.

With that the men went down into the waves. I saw Gary and John James himself joining the line, taking a hold of the rope and making their way out into the surf. Francis first turning sideways to take the waves, then as he disappeared from my sight, the next man, ten yards behind him, and on until there must have been six of them out there, ready to help the dinghy back in—if they were lucky, and didn't drown themselves, that is. And then I saw the dinghy with

22

Liam and Sean in it too. God knows how they stayed the right way up in that water. They couldn't get in close though. No way.

There was a horrid grinding and then a crack like a tooth splitting in your head. 'That's it!' Ian yelled. 'Her hull is gone.'

They'd all drown, every one of them.

Ian leaned closer to me. 'What's that?'

I shook my head. I had to keep them all in sight: the men on the line; Liam and Sean in the dinghy. If I lost them, they'd drown. That's what I thought. And their faces would stare pale and blank-eyed out of the black of my dreams, night after night with all those others . . .

Somewhere I heard Ian shouting at me to keep back, but that was when I saw the helmsman, poised for a moment up on the edge of his cockpit. He seemed so close I could see his face, black it was, black as your hat. He glanced over his shoulder, timing his jump maybe. Then he was gone. I could see heads bobbing in the water, but there seemed to be nothing but the sucking roar of the waves scrawing back at the strand.

Perhaps I was closer than I thought, for suddenly my legs were sucked right out from under me and I was down and thrashing like a fish in a net, desperate to get up and out. Another wave crashed into my back just as I found my feet and then I was in only a couple of inches. I think I was almost blubbering. Then there was another wave and I was up to my waist again.

Someone took my arm. 'Jesus, Willie, what are you playing at?' I looked up and there was Gary. 'No point in throwing yourself into the sea like that,' he said, smiling, and he hauled me up and held me steady.

'He didn't.' John James stepped up beside us. 'Kept himself well back, the little hero.'

Then there was a shout that the line was coming in and

both Gary and John pushed into the sea to help Mick steady the line, and bring them all in. I thought I saw Ian running in too, and then the men coming back, one after the other, hauling the line over their bent backs, like gods hauling in the very ocean, and Mick Barratt steady as a mountain, midway down the line. And then there was the dinghy, Ian hanging on its side, and, last of all, Francis and the lone dark-faced sailor.

We should have cheered, but there was none of that. I reckon every one of us was too thankful that there had been no life lost. Someone produced a bottle of whiskey and handed it round.

I saw the sailor having a rug pulled round his shoulders and being half carried, half led up to a car. The men began to disperse, drifting back up to the road. A small group, Ian and myself included, stayed on the beach. I don't know why, I could hardly feel my hands, but there was something in the way that boat was stuck there, keeled over, her fore jib in tatters, flapping loose like washing on the line, waves rolling over her, not so bad now that the tide was running out.

'All right, lads. Had enough excitement have you? For the one night, that is.' Gary patted Ian on the back. 'You've been a busy man.' And he laughed.

John passed by. 'Good man, Ian,' he said. 'No hard feelings, now. You could maybe teach our Willie a thing or two.'

Ian ignored him. 'You all right?' he said to me.

I wiped the bitter salt from my mouth. 'I'll do.'

'Never a sailor though?'

'Not in this life.'

He laughed and put an arm across my shoulder. He's a good butty, Ian is.

Gary came back from the group of men standing by the sailor, his wet jacket slung casually over a shoulder. 'Come on. John has his rented car up there.'

24

He was all right, Gary.

I might have thought different about John James too; after all he was one of the men who'd just risked their lives. But then, as we pulled up in front of the house, he said, 'Jesus Christ, lads, to think of all that fuss for a black fella.' And he shook his head and laughed.

'What are you on about?' Gary said, sort of sharpish.

'Didn't you see?' said John James. 'Didn't you see that the skipper was a darkie, you know. What the hell was he doing in a sailing boat in the first place? Jayz, what a waste of time.'

Gary glanced at me, shrugged and then looked out of the window. I didn't say anything. I don't think Ian even noticed. 'Ah well,' said John, 'what the hell. It passes the time, eh.' And he started to whistle to himself.

Three

Their faces are maggot pale in the darkness that I know is deep water. Their wrists are bone and their hands, long and skinny, move slowly, drifting up from the kelp weed, beckoning . . .

'Where are you off to, Willie?' My mother glanced past me into the front room. 'Jesus, Mary, and Joseph! Will you straighten the room. You'd think an army slept here. And we have visitors!'

Visitors? It's only the brothers, but I have more wit than to say as much. And as for sleep . . .

'Come back here! I said where do you think you're going? You'd drive a body demented.'

'Out.' Anyone else apart from my mother might think it a kindness on my part that I gave over my room to the two brothers and spent the night on what we call 'the good chair' in the front room.

'Come here to me.'

All the women in my family give instructions, from my mother down to Jeanie, and in the long run 'tis best to do as you're told, that's what I've found. I turned back from the door and stood in front of her. She's littler than me, her hair sort of ginger, but I reckon the colour comes from bottles for they're forever stacked up in our bathroom. I don't know why she bothers for she's hardly that old. My dad has plenty of years on her and so does Brede.

'You don't look so good,' she said. 'Are you sick?'

That took me by surprise. 'No. Ian and I never picked up

26

our money from Mick Barratt last night because of the boat and the rescue and all.'

She let go my wrist. 'Oh, that. Well, mind you're here this evening. I want to do a meal for the boys, early before they go out.'

'Sure.'

'And you'll tidy this room when you come back?'

'Yes, Mum.'

The wind had died away and the sky had that washed-out look, like it always does after a storm. And everything was running with wet and battered looking.

'Calm day, thank God.'

Old Tony Lavelle passed me by, with a friendly nod, and a question about the returned refugees, which is what he calls everyone who emigrates and then comes back for a visit. He has the little house nearest the shore and keeps cattle out on Inishkea North. Ian sometimes goes out with him in his boat but he's getting on and he talks of selling his land out there. He has no children, and his only brother is a policeman, a sergeant in the gardai down in Westport.

Ian and his Aunt Brede's cottage is up a little track from our lane. She has no money at all, Brede, but she keeps her place neat as a pin, the walls painted white each year and the tin roof red. Ian and herself fight a running battle with each other but I think it's only noise, for he's always after doing things for her, and she treats him like he was her own son.

Ian never talks about his real mother. She ran off shortly after he was born, ran off with a man from Achill, off to Dublin the pair of them and was never heard of again. Nobody knows who his father was. My mother says it could be any of the men out here she was that hot, but that's just my mother, I reckon. I remember her saying that and giving my da a hard look.

I think she was always worried that my father would run

27

away himself. I don't know why he doesn't, the insults she gives him, but he only smiles and tucks in on himself. Not a word she gets out of him when she's like that, though to be fair, she hardly gets a word out of him at the best of times. Families are complicated all right.

Auntie Brede was at the front of her house, feeding her hens. I always think she's fine looking, though Ian says there's something wrong with me when I tell him that. She's taller than many but thin. 'The handle of a shovel has a better figure than Brede,' my mother says but then there's always been the half sharp word between them. Don't ask me why.

I think she looks fine and solitary. There's a word. Solitary. Not lonely but strong in herself, not needing others—except maybe Ian. She can be sharp but more often than not she has a soft word, for me anyhow, and she's a crack. I think it's her eyes you notice first. It's not their colour, which is grey like her hair, but that they have a kind of sparkle in them.

'Good mornin', Willie. Fine day, thank God.'

It is a fact that we talk a lot about the weather out here but then why wouldn't we? There's an awful lot of sky and sea against our tiny little strip of land.

'Is he up?'

'Lord, yes. Been up this last hour or two. Some business. I don't know what. He hardly tells me anything at all . . . '

I smiled, for this was her usual complaint and Ian swore he told her everything. He could hardly fail to, he said, for she interrogated him more thoroughly than the security forces might. 'He told you nothing about the wreck last night?'

She sniffed dismissively. 'That old thing.' She took a handful of corn out of her jacket pocket and scattered it to the hens pecking around her feet. She always wore a man's jacket round the house. Her father's, she said it was. I'm not so sure; her father died over ten years ago. 'Was there really a dark fella on the yacht?' She tried not to sound interested.

'There was.'

'Poor wee fella,' she sighed. 'He must be a terrible long way from his home.'

'Did Ian say when he'd be back?'

'Of course not, but you are welcome to come in for a cup of tea and a slice of the cake I've made for your brothers. I don't expect you've had any breakfast.'

It's always hard with Brede. You know she has next to nothing but it would be hurtful to be forever saying no to her.

'Why would you be making cake for my brothers? You never liked them at all.'

'How dare you say that! I never minded that Gary too much, and it's for your poor mother I'm doing it anyway.' She didn't mention John James and nor did I. She could hardly have missed Ian's blackened eye this morning.

I settled into her kitchen by the window, and ate the slice of the fruit cake she put before me and drank a cup of tea and then had bread and a fresh egg. I hadn't realized how hungry I was. And we chatted. She loves to talk, and I like sitting there for she doesn't miss much that goes on in our village, and anyway, it's a great sight from Brede's window down to the half dozen cottages of Glosh, strung out along the winding lane. The little fields on either side, the few cattle, and then the land ending in a sharp slope, half cliff, down to the rocky shore. Then that ocean and, like great gleaming green whales humping out of the water, our two beautiful islands of Inishkea North and South. Sometimes they look so close you could almost step across to them, like the heroes of old would have had no trouble doing I'm sure.

It's a funny thing but I am happier here than in my own kitchen; maybe it's because there are no children. 'Why did you never marry, Brede?'

'And you think I still couldn't?'

It's true she's not old, really. 'Who do you have your eye on, then?'

'You mind your manners, William Michael.' Michael's my father's name. She's the only person who ever calls me that, and then only when she's ticking me off.

Ian came banging in about half an hour later. Not in a good temper.

'Well?' I asked. 'Were you off at Mick Barratt's?' Ian is a fierce man for the money. He'd run a mile for a pound.

'A fiver between the two of us because we only did half the job. Says we can go back and finish off if we want the rest.'

I shrugged. It was more than I expected.

'That bloody man is tighter than a pig's belly.'

'Mind your language, Ian,' said Brede and poured him a tea.

'Aye, well, he promised us.' He slumped into the chair beside me and helped himself to a piece of the cake. I have to say it gave me a sneaky pleasure to be eating the cake set aside for my brothers, like eating the fattened calf before the prodigal got back. I never had too much time for that prodigal son and his doting father. Father Paul comes out with it every Christmas and August when the emigrants all come back.

'And you lost your temper again.'

'I don't like your brother.'

'It's more you like Anna too much.'

Brede laughed. 'He's moony over her.'

'She'll run away with me before she'd ever look at you,' I said.

'Ach, you're a dreamer boy. But I tell you what, the Macbraids have taken in that fella we hauled off the boat. It's the talk of the village, and he's not hurt or nothing but starved they say. What do you say we go and have a look at

30

the wreck? I have a bit of a plan. John James won't be too pleased; Anna waiting on the black fella. You heard what he said last night.'

'He was always a bigot, that boy,' said Brede. 'No tolerance for anyone who isn't from here, or who's different from himself.'

'That's him,' I agreed. I glanced at Ian.

There were quite a few people on the shore when we cycled up, and I reckoned there would be many for a month or more. It was just that way when a young whale was washed up on the opposite side of this beach here, the Atlantic side we call it. It was in the spring, the poor thing was stranded, sick it must have been, and whole families came and picnicked beside it until it began to smell. Then the council cut it up and took it away, bones and all.

We drifted by the small groups standing beside their cars.

'Fine looking boat, isn't she?'

'Hardly that big though.'

'Came all the way from Africa.'

'That's a fair distance. You wouldn't catch me sailing that far, not in a boat that size.'

'What are you talking about, Paddy? You have only ever been to Castlebar once in your life and you've never set foot in a boat at all.'

'Well, that's not to say I mightn't.'

Sure everyone would come and look, and they would come back too.

Ian was silent, studying the boat carefully. The storm had driven her hard up into the shallow water last night and now she lay beam on to the beach about thirty yards out, heeled over. 'You would be almost able to walk out to her dry footed at low tide,' Ian said. 'Anybody could walk aboard her then.'

'Ah, no one would do that.'

'Maybe not. But look at her, Willie, she's not a bad yacht at all, there's fancy fittings, brass. She must have cost a lot of money.'

We watched some children trying to wade out to her, but the water was cold, and too deep for them. They got out as far as their waists, and then with a deal of shouting and yelling they came back in again.

'What do you say we have a closer look, maybe later when the tide is out and there aren't so many people around?'

I looked at him. 'What are you saying?'

'Just to look.'

We made our way back to Barratt's bar, where Mick made us wash the floor and shift chairs and scuttle about for a good hour before he paid us the rest of our money. I didn't mind; I reckon he's a good sort, Mick. There is something safe about him, about the way he anchored those men last night, holding the rope while they forged out into the surf. And he isn't a man to get cross over nothing. All he said to Ian was, 'How's the sight?' referring to his black eye.

'It'll do,' said Ian.

He knew Ian was soft on Anna. He knew most things, but then I suppose in a place like ours it's likely that everybody knows what's going on, not just in their own village but in the two or three around them as well. I like to keep things to myself a bit; I think those of us from the islands are like that. Anyway Mick asked us whether we would deliver groceries up to the Macbraids' house—the other side of the pub is a shop, which is the way with a good lot of the drinking places here.

'All right,' said Ian. Then to me, 'I'll manage it on my own, Willie.'

Mick smiled.

I said, 'You will not. We'll carry the messages together; that or you'll be getting another black eye.'

In fact there were only a couple of packages so he could have carried them on his own, but what the hell: he may have just wanted to have a gaze at Anna but I wanted to talk to the sailor, if I got a chance, that was.

Four

'Hello, Willie.'

'How're ya, Anna?'

Put me in front of Anna Macbraid and I'm right stupid. I can hardly find a single word to say at all. Not so foolish, mind, that I didn't notice how she ignored Ian bobbing up and down beside me.

'Anna,' he said, 'God, you look great. Where'll you want the groceries?' And he was halfway in through the door already.

'I'll take them.'

'And mine,' I said, holding out the cardboard box filled mostly with milk and oat cereal. 'Will I balance it on top of Ian's?'

She smiled and pushed back a stray lock of black hair with her wrist. I love the way she does that. Little gestures can drive you wild, I reckon.

'No, Willie, would you ever bring them through into the kitchen.' I squeezed past. Well, there's favouritism for you. 'And you can wait outside, Ian Carey. We don't want you picking a fight or yelling your head off, not with our guest, thank you.'

'What are you going on about—?' But Ian's protest was cut short. She shut the door in his face. Cruel, wasn't it? I had to laugh all the same, and she gave me another great smile as soon as she had done it.

'He gets fierce uppity that friend of yours, doesn't he?'

I was tempted to say he was no friend of mine at all for I'd read somewhere that all's fair in love and war, but it seemed a bit hard, and anyway it was a lie. Instead I found myself telling her how some wouldn't think so badly of him as he was one of those who'd gone into the sea to rescue the sailor.

'Was he now?' she said, smiling again. She has a kind of a dark-eyed smile, sleepy and sideways. It would kill you. It really would. 'I hear your brother was mighty altogether.'

So that was it. John James didn't waste much time, did he. 'You mean Gary,' I said.

'Oh, him too.'

'I wouldn't know about John James.' I slapped the groceries down on the kitchen table, said hello to her mother.

Mrs Macbraid offered me a Coke, so I had one and asked her about their sailor. 'Ian reckons he must be rich sailing a yacht big as that.'

'You would think the man was a prince of Africa the number of callers we've had wanting to know about him,' said Mrs Macbraid.

'If he's a prince, he's a terrible skinny one,' said Anna.

'Jesus, Mary, and Joseph!' exclaimed Mrs Macbraid. 'Were ye spying on a naked man?'

Her granny cackled and winked at me. Anyone could tell she doted on the girl.

'He was not naked and I was not peering . . . '

The truth was they had found out little about him, for he had slept most of the day, and eaten little. His name was Malouf. According to the mother, he had a fever most likely and wouldn't be out of his bed for a few days.

I said my goodbyes and went out to find that Ian had gone off, probably down to the harbour at Blacksod. I'd told him about the family meal my mother was putting on; everybody in our village would be invited in, so I'd see him there. I made my way

35

slowly back to Glosh, wheeling the bike because I felt too lazy to cycle uphill.

My mother had her party for the brothers, and all our neighbours came. There was a regular mountain of food, of course, as if John James and Gary hadn't eaten a decent meal in all the years they'd been away. And there was drink too, which Gary helped himself to; not John though, he's the careful man right enough; keeps himself trim, works out in a gym and belongs to a tennis club.

And to hear John talk you'd say he was on the pig's back all right. To me he's like those smooth men in the telly ads. Fake, you know. I heard a neighbour saying he could've been a politician, the way he talked. Sure, everyone is entitled to make a million and become president of the United States. Why should I care?

I'll tell you. Because I reckoned that behind the charm there was a sneer for all of us who lived back here at the end of the western world, as he put it. I heard it and I knew Ian heard it, too, but he has more wit than myself and busied himself away out of the room, chatting to old Tony Lavelle and to my sister Mary who for some strange reason has always made a bit of a pet of Ian.

No one else minded John James at all, certainly not my mother; he could fart black wind and she would reckon it singing.

'No, of course this place is beautiful,' John James was saying, 'and there sure is nowhere like it, not in Chicago anyhows.' That got a laugh. 'But you can see, anyone can see, that there's no work here, no prospects at all. Why else is it that all those with a bit of get-up-and-go—you know what I mean . . .'

I had to back away in case I threw up all over the cake I was handing round.

' . . . leave. And I tell you there are plenty from the Mullet, from Erris, who've made a lot of money in the States. A lot of money.'

Ian should be hearing this, that's what I was thinking. Except I knew that he would never emigrate to the States, not while my brother was living there. He wouldn't like the prospect of bumping into him.

'Ah, you're right, John,' they chimed in one after the other. We can be great at moaning out here, that's a fact.

'It's desperate land here, hungry land.' This was Jim Deane. He had more cattle than the rest of the village and was a hard-working soul. 'No good in the soil for farming and the sea is a curse.'

'That's just what I'm saying!' said John. He's acquired a phoney accent and all.

'And what do you think we should do then, John James? All move to America?'

'Not at all. But I reckon you could realize some assets here maybe with a bit of careful handling.'

I saw he was looking out of the window when he was saying this, and I wondered what slick deal was forming in his head.

A little later I heard him asking Jim how much land he had out on the islands.

'Maybe forty acre or so,' the farmer replied. ' 'Bout the same, maybe less than your dad.'

Gary winked and gave me a nudge. 'That man knows how much land he has down to the last square inch.' Indeed he does but then so does everyone else here. We're all much the same when it comes to land. Of course I don't have a scrap that's my own but maybe one day I will. I would like that, and I reckon I would hold on to it, and try to make it work for me too.

Jim must have overheard Gary for he looked him right in the eye. 'Well, Gary,' he said, 'you were always the boyo.'

'Ever since I put on my first pair of long trousers I was,' smiled Gary. His breath smelt of beer.

I drifted out to the kitchen where Dad was holding court with Brede and a couple of blow-ins from Aghleam. They were talking about the stranded sailor; that African fella, Dad kept calling him. That's what anyone with a darker skin is called round these parts. Not that I'd seen someone so different in looks, apart from on the television, of course, until I saw that poor fella hunkered down in the cockpit of his floundering yacht.

'North Africa.'

'A long way from home.'

'Well,' said my father, taking out a pack of ten Sweet Afton, 'I tell you what I think.'

'And what would that be?'

My father paused as he always did when he was settling in to a good conversation, cupping his hands round the lighted match as if he were out on the open sea. 'I think that that man is no right man at all.'

'What're you talking about?' said Brede dismissively. 'What the divil is he if he is not a man? I suppose you'll be saying he's from Mars. Is that it, you hopeless man?'

I think he liked stirring up Brede. He looked her straight in the eye, and there was not a flicker of a smile on his face when he said, 'I would say he was the stranger from the west.'

She shook her head and turned away. 'Your brain is coddled,' she said.

'It is not,' said my father. 'That man will raise the godstone,' he said, striking the flat of his hand against the table, 'and put rest on the island.'

You can never tell with my dad when exactly he's being serious or not. Brede gave a huff and went off to help my mother with the sandwiches. But there were others there with whom the idea somehow struck a bit of a chord.

38

Old Tony was at the door when my father was battering on. He nodded and said, 'God rest their souls.' Everyone knew he was talking about the drowned men of '27. 'Sure if this man found the godstone and settled their troubled sleep it would be a blessed thing.'

'It would.'

Then someone cracked a joke about it only being the spirit talking, meaning the Paddy's my dad was drinking, and the little group laughed and the chat moved on to other things but it left me thinking.

I didn't often hear my father talking about such things but he was quite a scholar and knew all there was to know about the islands. We had characters all the way from Dublin come to talk to him and record what he had to say, and his telling of the stories. I had heard of the godstone, we all had. It had been kept on the south island for centuries, long before the monks came west.

Shaped a bit like the head of a man, it had been brought out for every ceremony, every birth, death, and marriage and, so the story goes, the islanders would fare well for as long as they kept the stone. But they feared it would be lost for that was the story too, and only after long hard years would a stranger from the west come, one of the fair folk, and he would find the stone and set things to rest.

And you know what they meant by that? Fairies. It would make you laugh seeing grown men believe in such things. But though they pretended, I know my dad and his closest pals do believe in some odd corner of their minds that there are the blessed isles or Tir na Nog as they are called, and that there was a time in this land when the fair folk mixed with mortals such as us.

Well, the godstone was lost, not in my father's time but not so long before it either. And ever since then, and I know this is fact, life on the islands became harder and harder until the black storm of '27, when all the young men were drowned.

That's what my dream is about: the black storm and the voices and the hands reaching and reaching up to me, all those men back then, when my dad was a wee fella, all drowned and rolling to and fro in the deep water, restless and lost.

Sometimes I think it's not so much drowning that gives me such terror, but the dead men, all the poor dead drowned souls somehow waiting for me. Makes no sense I know, but there it is.

'Ye're dreaming, Willie,' said Ian coming and sitting himself beside me.

'I am not.'

'Who're you kiddin'?' he said, shovelling the last piece of cake into his mouth. 'Did you hear what John said when your dad was talking?'

'No.'

'He said that poor sailor was bound to turn out a thief or worse and only in a daft spot such as this would we even bother to give such a man shelter and help, let alone believe he was some creature out of a long dead story.'

I didn't bother to answer and Ian didn't say anything else until our neighbours started to drift off and he and I strolled down the lane to the high field above the shore, to watch the sun going down, in a long streak of orange and gold. Times like that it's not so hard to believe along with my dad and the old ones that there's something out there, beyond the edge of the ocean, another world altogether.

Ian's mind was on other things, though. 'I reckon we should look over the yacht. What do you say, Willie? Now would be the time. The tide will be well out. We'll be able to walk out to it.'

'What would we want to be going on to that man's boat for?'

40

'Why, to see if your dad is right. Sure, if he comes from the blessed isles it'll all be in the ship's log.'

I hit him, of course, but I knew what he was really saying: that it would be interesting to see whether there could be a grain of truth in what John James had hinted, that this skipper was not the rightful owner of the yacht he was sailing. That would be a thing all right for there might be a reward then—that would be Ian's thinking, but I was no better than him.

Neither of us had the courage or decency to come out and say what was on our minds for it was shameful to think it, knowing that if the man had been white and speaking Dutch or German we would never have doubted him at all.

Five

That night was the first time we clambered on to that African's boat. I knew it was wrong, but not in the way that it would do anyone any harm, not to the sailor anyhow. He wasn't going to know about it, and nor was anyone else. After the party nobody minded what I got up to. The lads and my dad, and my mother this time, had gone off drinking, so Ian and I took our bikes and cycled to Elly Bay.

There was a good moon still and when we walked down on to the strand we could see the boat there, out in the calm, shallow water, tilted on her side like an 'auld' one after a pint too many. And it was so quiet you could hear a car coming a mile off. But there was no reason to hide or be skulking about—there was no one stopping to have a look at this hour and no gardai patrolling. We had the bay to ourselves.

Now when the sea's like this you'd think I wouldn't mind it at all. There's hardly a fear of getting drowned just wading out no deeper than your waist, and good level sand under foot. That's what you'd think.

Without a word Ian stripped off his jeans, rolled them up and dropped them on the dry sand.

'Well?'

'What?'

'Christ, Willie, are you coming or what?' He jigged up and down on his toes, always impatient. 'Come on.' He started to run.

It was not going to be that bad. Not like in the storm. I could do it. If I forced myself. I stripped and scuttled after him. I'm not the world's greatest sprinter but I can keep going for a long while, if I need to. There was a race from one end of the Mullet right the way to Belmullet at the other end. I did all right, finished third. Of course, all my mates who ran and then stopped off at Phelan's pub halfway said they could have done it easy if they hadn't got so thirsty. Ah, but they're all talk mostly.

I went straight in. Water is slimy and that's a fact. I don't mind it being freezing; it's the sliminess of it I hate, slick all around your ankles. I tried telling Mary this and she said I was cracked. She listed all the things she reckoned were slimy: jellyfish, seaweed, wet mud. There you go, I said to her, that's all sea stuff. And you can't tell me the sea's not alive. Jesus, there are enough living things under that skin of green to convince me it's alive, and wanting to pull you in.

That night I could feel the grip of it and it made my breathing peculiar, sort of catching at my chest. God, it was a long haul out to the boat. But the water was shallow and, I kept telling myself, there was no way a drowned body could be waiting for me.

Ian was at the hull. I saw the dark outline of his body at the rail, maybe looking back to me, and then he slipped edgeways round the stern and was out of sight.

I was doing all right, there was nothing but the swish of the water around my waist, my hands were up in the air, over my head you know, kind of keeping balance. Nothing had touched my foot and I hadn't yelled or anything. Ian knew how I felt. I say he knew because I had told him often enough, but sometimes I think that though he's my best friend, he's not got the greatest imagination in the world. Because he likes slopping about in boats he secretly believes I'm half putting it on, but the truth is only folk who go to sea drown.

I tried talking to my da about it one time but he just interrupted me and said, 'I know all about that,' way before I had got a chance to tell him half of it.

I counted the steps I had to take: twenty, twenty-one . . . and then I was there. 'Where are you?' I hissed.

'Here. Stop fussing will you.' Ian emerged from the shadows and pointed. I could just make out the letters on her stern in the thin moonlight. *Katya* and then in small thick black letters her country of registration: *Deutschland*.

'That's never an African country,' whispered Ian.

'Isn't it?'

'No.'

'Well, what is it then?'

We were hissing at each other like a pair of cats.

'I don't know, German, maybe, but I told you there was something queer about it.'

'Why shouldn't he be having a German-made boat?' I asked.

'Don't be stupid.'

I shrugged. I wanted to get out of the sea, that was what I wanted, and if he was that convinced then surely he was right. To be honest I didn't care. We slithered up the port side, like a pair of oversized Mayo rats, for her rails were down in the water there. No problem. Then we hand-hauled ourselves along and into the cockpit, still awash from the storm of the night before, and there we paused and looked at each other. It was strange us being tilted over sideways like that, like a dream almost.

'She's ruined, isn't she?' I said. 'Never sail again.'

'I don't know. I don't see why not. A good-sized cockpit, hasn't she? Could have held four or maybe five men easy, and yet there was only himself.' That seemed to bother Ian. He took the wheel and stood leaning against it, as if he were imagining sailing her.

'She feels dead to me.'

'What do you know?'

'I know enough.' Friends can get on your nerves same as other people.

'Why do you think he was on his own, Will?'

'Maybe he didn't start the journey on his own.' That was a thought . . .

'Murder, maybe?' I could tell he liked that idea. Murder. Piracy on the high seas. Ian hadn't changed much since he was seven and I had to tell him the story of *Treasure Island* that Mary had just told to me. I had to tell him it seventeen times. I counted it and wrote it in my diary.

'She certainly would have cost a lot, serious money,' he said. And he said it in such a way you'd think he had already found that poor skipper not only guilty of committing murder but robbery to boot.

'Ah, go away, Ian. You're sick in the head.'

He ignored that. 'Look at this—the winding gear. Never seen stuff like that. I reckon it's so you could sail single handed.'

'Well done, professor. We all saw him sailing her single handed, didn't we? You've cleared him of murder so. Ian, what the hell are we doing out here, just tell me that?'

'Frightened?'

God, the number of things I'm forever having to do just so that I can pretend I'm not frightened. I tell you it's what'll kill me. Only thing that keeps me sane is I reckon everybody else must be much the same, apart from Ian who doesn't have the brain to be frightened when he ought.

'We'll not find out anything sitting up here,' I said. 'Try the hatch.' I presumed it would be locked in which case honour would have been satisfied and we could have gone home. My bed, or at least the armchair in the parlour, seemed distinctly inviting.

But the hatch slid open, smooth as grease. And there we were on this wrecked boat, the skipper taking shelter in our village, and us looking down into the dark throat of the companionway. 'Isn't that handy,' Ian said, and grinned. 'What we've got to do is look for the papers, ship's papers.'

We were stupid, of course, for we had no light, so we blundered about until I fair cursed him and said that I was not going to crack myself one more time and he could stay there if he liked but I was for leaving.

We left, carefully closing the hatch behind us.

It was eleven by the time we were back at the village. 'Tomorrow,' said Ian. 'All right? And we'll bring a couple of torches. Nice boat, you know, Willie. Expensive fittings.'

'You sound like a dentist,' I said.

'You don't have to come.'

'Oh?'

I knew the way his mind was working. 'You think you'll make some money, don't you, tight bastard.'

'Reward,' he said. 'Bound to be. I'll swear that fella stole it. A couple of grand reward, Will, what would you say to that?'

Two thousand pounds between us. Jesus, with that sort of money you could be a different person. I'd make a room of my own, is what I would do.

'Hey, Anna might be impressed, mightn't she?'

Indeed she might. I had a bit of a feeling that Anna might be on the lookout for a millionaire and not two under-age scruffs from Blacksod.

The next night I was ready to go out again. More tricky because all the family were in and I had to wait till they were asleep. But I waited, and a little after midnight I was up outside Ian's. I gave a low whistle and a few minutes later I saw his dark shadow slipping away round the corner of the house and then coming down to me.

Once again we had no trouble wading out to the yacht and once again I felt like a thief slithering crabwise along the tilting deck and into the cockpit. We slid the hatch open, and then with Ian leading the way, we climbed down. He clicked on the torch and slowly passed the beam all the way round the saloon.

I had never seen anything so beautiful. It was dark and rich with money and time having been spent on it. All wood and fine handles, snug and spacious. I could have lived there easy, I really could.

In one corner was a chart table with a map of our bit of the coast set out on it and all sorts of radio stuff that Ian was familiar with, but which meant nothing to me.

'Serious boat this,' he kept saying as if some yachts would maybe crack a joke when you looked over them.

He wasn't such a tidy man himself though, our shipwrecked skipper; there were oilskins on the side, wetting everything, and to the left, facing up to the bow there was a cabin door wedged open and I could see the bed, scuffled with bits of clothing and rumpled blankets, and on the side little cups, dirty.

Ian went in, nosing like a hound while I drifted through the other door on the right which led up past one cabin and a second, through to the littlest kitchen—a galley, Ian called it—that you ever saw. That was a mess and all, and then beyond that a bathroom, the size of a coffin stood up on its end.

All small enough, maybe, but apart from the skim of mess your man had left over most things, it was perfect and classy. The doors clunked closed soft and solid at the same time, and there was space for everything you might need, lockers and drawers and the devil knows what.

I thought I heard a soft knock against the hull. 'Was that you, Ian?'

No answer. I ignored it. Just that slight swell slapping up against the stationary boat.

I turned on a ring on the stove and there was a hiss of gas escaping. No problem with the old cooked breakfast, I thought. God, wouldn't you need something like that if you were sailing up from Africa, if that was where he had come from.

'Hey! I've got it. The book.' I hurried back to the saloon, where Ian was pouring over a leather-bound volume, torch in one hand following the text with the other. 'Stengart. That's the owner's name. Bikel Stengart.' He looked up at me. 'Don't tell me that weasel's ever called by a name like that.'

He had a point.

I said, 'I reckon we tell Francis, what do you say?'

'You must be joking. I tell you, we got to think this out otherwise we'll get nothing out of it all. Maybe we should phone this Stengart or something.'

'You know how to speak German, Ian?' What an idiot.

'I speak German!' barked a voice out of the darkness.

'Jesus!' I practically jumped right out of my skin. There was this fella, his face a black round blob in the hatchway, eyes in the torchlight huge and white, and teeth. Eyes and teeth.

'I speak English!' He sounded excited and angry. I didn't blame him. I wished I wasn't there.

Six

I was that frightened I couldn't say anything at all, nor Ian.
A couple of mutes we were. I could hear the man breathing
above us and then Ian swallowing. 'Christ,' he whispered,
'it's the black skipper.'

Aren't you the bloody scholar! I thought. Who the hell
else would be out there apart from eejits like us, and the
skipper from Africa himself?

'I speak English. God damn!' The skipper's voice was
pitched oddly, a little high, no mistaking the anger though.

'We're sorry, mister,' I said, reckoning an apology was a
fair way to begin getting ourselves out of this. It wasn't.

'Thief!' He just about shrieked the word at us and
swung down the companion, not touching the steps at all
and landing lightly on the balls of his feet, a dark shape in
the darkness, hunched, legs bent. I took a step back and
Ian, as taken by surprise as myself, swung the torch on
him.

'Turn it off or I bite your head—God damn!'

With his eyes white and rolling about in that dark face, I
tell you he looked frightening and I cursed Ian for an idiot
persuading me to go skittering about in the dark, boarding
this boat. I gave Ian a poke in the side. 'Tell him we didn't
mean anything at all.'

But before Ian could open his mouth, the man leaned
forward. 'Two thief!' He snapped his finger under Ian's
nose. 'Two thief. Irish thief.' And then a stream of his own
strange language—all hoarse and spitty it was too, and I
couldn't help feeling that he was describing some terrible
punishment that I think involved poking our eyeballs out,

49

because he kept jabbing first at his own eyes, grimacing, and then stabbing them at Ian.

'Do that again, mister . . . ' faltered Ian, 'and we'll . . . '

We would do nothing at all and that was a fact.

'Oh yes, thief, speak English. What you steal, thief? What you steal from my boat. Hey!' He made a sudden jerk with his hand, sideways and I caught a flash of metal in the torchlight.

God knows where it had come from but there it was, a wicked little knife, snug in the palm of his hand. Ian snapped his head back and cracked himself against the bulwark, and down he went like a sack of potatoes. I could've cursed him, leaving me right in it, on me own.

'Jesus, mind that,' I said holding up my hands, palms towards him to show that I didn't mean any harm. 'Just looking. She's a fine boat, and we . . . er . . . '

'It is night,' he hissed. 'Night time for thieves, not for looking.'

'You have a point there,' I agreed, 'but it was a bit of a lark you know, an adventure.' I chatted on in what I hoped was a peace-making fashion.

Sister Mairaid said I could talk the hind legs off a donkey when I had a mind to do it. She meant that I half drove her crazy one time when I wanted to wangle my way on to a coach trip to Galway, and she ended up letting me just to shut me up.

Your man here had his head cocked on one side as if half listening to me and half listening to whatever might be outside the boat. I hoped there was nothing there. It was crowded enough below decks and I didn't fancy having to do any more explaining.

' . . . And you see Ian here is just crazy about boats and well . . . Maybe I had better get him out,' I said, and did a mime of hauling Ian out by the scruff of his neck and nodding up at the companionway, through which I could see a single brilliant star.

He stooped, grabbed Ian's chin and, before I could stop him, waggled it to and fro, grunted, took the torch out of Ian's hand, and then stood up again. Obviously he reckoned nothing was broken, which was a relief. He glanced at the torch and hooked it up on the ceiling, where it hung at an angle, casting a thin spotlight down on to Ian's legs. 'Who you?'

We stood there facing each other, the pool of light between us. 'Nobody at all,' I said in answer to his question. 'That is, nobody important, you know.'

'Hah!'

'My name is Willie Cormack.' I said it slow and clear so he would hear it right. I never like people to get me name wrong. I don't know what it is, but I don't like it. Funny thing was but it was either in the sound of my name or in the manner of my saying it, but something impressed him a little, well enough to take the heat out of his manner. 'I know Anna,' I added. 'Anna Macbraid, the one you're staying with.' Maybe that wasn't so wise, for he would surely tell her and she wouldn't be so pleased.

'Anna! Ah.' He nodded. Then he said it again. 'Anna.'

'That's right,' said I. And I don't know what possessed me, there was Ian out for the count, there was this character odder than a pair of left-footed boots with a knife in his hand, and all of us tilted sideways like so many drunken sailors, and I said: 'I'm going to marry her and all.' He understood all right for he kind of fixed me with his eyes, staring.

'Yeah, well, I reckon I ought to shift this lad.'

'No!'

That was a mistake on my part. But at least he wasn't dancing about like fury any longer, making his witching jabs or shaking his knife in my face. 'All right,' I said. 'I tell you what. You check to see if anything's missing, and then we'll go. How's that?'

He nodded slowly, glanced around the saloon, unhooked the torch and flashed it into his cabin and then down the passage to the galley. I kept still, then he shone the torch on me, then down on Ian and then I heard the intake of his breath. 'So . . . ' There was the ship's registration book lying on the ground where it had fallen out of Ian's hand. 'You want to thief my boat?'

'No, of course not . . . but it's not your boat anyhow, is it?' I don't know why I said that. I think the danger had somehow gone out of the moment and I was chancing my arm, just wanted to know what he would say. 'Bikel Stengart is the owner, is that right?'

He looked at me and I swear there was the beginning of tears welling up in his eyes. All of a sudden he said, 'Go!' real sharp. 'Go! Go!'

'All right. No problem.' I hoiked Ian into a sitting position. He groaned. 'Come on,' I urged him. 'We're not entirely welcome.'

'My head. I think it's split in half.'

'Never mind that. Just get up.' Somehow I hustled him to the companionway, and half pushed him up into the cockpit. 'OK,' I said to the skipper, 'we're on our way. I don't suppose we could have the torch back, could we?'

He made no response.

'Fair enough,' I said and nipped up the ladder before he changed his mind and slit my throat after all. And then from the safety of the cockpit, I poked my head back through the hatchway and said, 'Tell me one thing now, who's Bikel Stengart?'

He didn't answer straight off but took the torch down and shone it up at me, full in my face, blinding me. 'Dead man.' I didn't know if it was a threat to me, or whether he was talking about the registered owner, but I reckoned it was time to make off.

The night air must have cleared Ian's head, for he was

standing at the rail waiting for me. 'What was that about?' he said.

'I'll tell you later. Go on, and I'll follow you.'

He slid down into the sea, and, gritting my teeth, I followed. We didn't talk until we were ashore, and then my teeth started chattering so bad I could hardly talk at all. It wasn't until we were cycling back up to Aghleam that I felt the blood coming back into my frozen arms and legs. Then I told him what had passed.

'You didn't get much out of him,' he said. Which was sort of cheeky considering how he had failed altogether. 'But then maybe we were lucky. He was probably a murderer, Willie. Did you see the knife he tried to cut me with?'

'Ah, he was only waving it about.' I didn't want him to start dressing up the incident into something it wasn't. 'And we were trespassing, remember. I think we should tell Francis.'

Reluctantly Ian agreed—Francis would understand all that stuff about the registration, though I was a little nervous as to how we were going to explain how we came to be on the African's boat in the first place.

I crept into our house through the kitchen. There was no sound from anywhere apart from snoring from my bedroom. I stretched out my sleeping bag on the floor of the parlour and went to sleep and I dreamed that dream again.

Do you ever recall that story of the Israelites being chased across the sea by one of them Pharaoh's armies? I saw a picture of that scene one time and it stayed with me and became part of the dream. In the picture you could see all the army in their chariots, clattering over the sandy floor of the Red Sea with the water like a huge glass wall towering over them. And you could see into that wall of water and there were squid and giant crabs with their claws poking through the glass, and sharks, with eyes dead as tombs, and mouths gaping wide. And the sea and the creatures were so large and the men in their chariots were so tiny, you know. Well, there are bits of that in my dream all right, just bits, though none of your ancient Egyptians. I wouldn't have minded some company in my dream, living company that is, for the only people in it are the dead peering through that glassy wall . . .

'Jesus, Willie, what the hell are you at! Can't you let a man sleep?'

I often yell when I have the dream, and I wake sweating and coughing and finding it hard to catch my breath.

Gary, towel round his middle and hair over one eye and the black stubble on his chin, stood in the doorway. Behind him was movement, my mother passing by, going into the kitchen.

'Let him be, Gary,' she said.

'What was it? Not your old nightmares?' He scrubbed his chin. 'And what happened to your face? God, you're gushing.'

I touched my nose and peered at my hand. It came away sticky with blood. I suddenly realized how sore my whole face was. I know how I did it: I had jerked my head back to avoid 'it' grabbing my eye, and, lying on the floor by the chair, as I was, I must have whacked the leg of the chair right into my face, given myself a nosebleed.

'I'm OK,' I said and wadged my T-shirt up to my face and then edged past him and went down to the bathroom to clean myself up.

Dad was at the table when I came in. He hardly eats anything any more, just the cup of tea. But he likes to sit at the table for the length of a meal, even if it's breakfast. Not me, I like to get in and out, particularly with the boys home and there's hardly room to swing a cat.

Dad always looks starched and trim on a Sunday before mass, his cheeks shining from the razoring. Always the white collar too, and when he steps out of the door he wears an old, fine, felt hat, like you sometimes see in those black and white movies on the telly, that all the men wore in them days. No one looks quite like my father.

'You all right?' he said to me as I sat myself down.

'Sure.'

'That boy ought to see a psychowhatchamacall,' said my mother. 'Will you have a rasher, Jeanie?' Jeanie shook her head. 'And were you out last night?' said Mum, giving me a sharp look.

'You mean getting up in the night?' Blank innocence on my face—at least I hope that was my expression. 'I heard a noise round the shed. Thought it might be a fox.'

'Oh,' said my father. 'Eddie claimed he shot the fox that was bothering us all a couple of days back.'

'Maybe it was his ghost,' I said.

'Maybe it was.' He supped his tea and I thought he smiled to himself.

Jeanie pulled up the chair, wanting to know why we were talking about ghosts and did I know that there was blood on my face still. And then she took Patrick's spoon so there was mayhem and Mum had to pick him up and tuck him under her arm and cook with only one hand. Mary came in, and tried to take over from Mum but she insisted on seeing everyone fed.

'Suit yourself,' said Mary; she wasn't one for wasting words.

'Gary! John!' Mum called, putting Patrick back in his chair. 'Will you have a cooked breakfast?'

'The full lash,' said Gary.

I reckon she wants to get them so fat they won't fit aboard the plane at the end of their holidays.

I scooped up the last of my cereal and made way for Gary.

He was full of chat, and teased my mother, so that she was half laughing and half exasperated with him; it's nice the way he can do that. I'm not jealous that they get on. I'm not Gary, nor would ever want to be.

John James sauntered in well after the rest of us. God, you would think he was lord of all creation, and just because he had the hire of the car, and he knew we would all have to wait on him.

Dad nodded at me and Jeanie. 'We'll go on ahead, so,' he said. 'Catch a lift with Eddie. Mary can come too. Is that all right?'

'Of course,' said Mum. 'Off you go.' And then her attention was back on the eldest. 'Johnnie James, that is a fine suit. My word, are you after some poor lass's heart today or what is it, at all?'

John smiled.

Gary swigged his tea and wiped his mouth. 'Ach, he's too in love with himself to mind any girl from this village.'

'Oh, I don't know,' said John. 'That Anna Macbraid has turned into a fair good looker.'

I wanted to tell him to lay off her but that would only have stirred him, so I said nothing, just got up and followed Dad out of the house, slamming the door behind me.

The two girls joined the choir at the back of the church while Dad and I went up into the men's balcony. I slid along the pew and joined Ian.

'What happened to you?' he muttered from behind his hands.

'Banged me face on a chair.'

'Eejit.'

'You're no better.' And he wasn't either. I couldn't see the bump on his head, but there was a plaster on his cheek

56

where he had cut himself, falling, and he looked whiter than a ghost, with bags under his eyes too.

I watched my mother coming in, Gary and John behind her, both of them nodding away like royalty. Gary came up to join us, John stayed down below. It was funny how travel changes some and not others. I reckon Gary will remain a Mullet man for the rest of his life wherever he lives, but not John. He'd come back for the crack, maybe, or out of duty, but there was no real pull. I got the feeling he looked down on us all. Even the way he dressed was different.

Ian nudged me. In came the Macbraids, Anna wearing a red bomber jacket and looking like a queen. And God! There was the black fella beside her. We ducked.

It's not exactly noisy before mass starts but there's shuffling and a fair bit of whispering as neighbours acknowledge each other with a nod. But as the Macbraids walked up the aisle there was a kind of ripple running right across the church, heads all turning the one way. I saw John looking, more like scowling. Stupid man. Wasn't as if we never have strangers coming to us, visitors and such like. Though not that many who are washed up in a wild storm, I suppose, and are dark-skinned Africans at that.

I felt sorry for the man and thought it was only bad luck that he'd have to put up with our horse-riding priest for the next hour. I didn't think that would give much succour to a stranded seaman a thousand miles from his own shore.

Sure enough we had the same sermon as he'd come up with for the last two Sundays—his pension, or something like that. I'm away after the first two minutes looking at the little stained-glass window we have behind the altar. There he is, Jesus, out on Galilee calming the storm, just with the hand held out.

After mass my father went off to Barratt's bar for a pint, Gary with him, while John James ushered my mother and the girls into the car. 'You getting in, Willie?'

'No. I'm off with Ian.' It was a fair old hike up to Francis's but there was no harm, it was a fine day.

I don't know where Anna had got to but I saw the skipper at the church door having a bit of an altercation with Father Paul. A group of men were standing nearby, half watching, one or two of them smiling. The African was waving his arms about while Father Paul's face was looking so hot you could fry an egg on it.

'What's that about?' I said to Ian.

'Who cares. He's always having a go at someone.'

Ailish King and her best friend, Jean Coyle, came up to us, the two of them sputtering with the giggles. 'Father didn't like him having a swig of the altar wine,' said Jean.

'Only 'cause he wanted to keep it for his own dinner,' said Ailish. 'See you round, boys.' And the two of them were off, howling like mad ones; you wouldn't know why really.

Francis's wife opened the door to us and brought us into the kitchen where himself was sitting at the table reading the *Sunday Tribune*. 'What's up, lads?' he said.

Ian did the talking. He skated over the bit about us boarding *Katya*, then he asked about the registration book.

'If it were stolen and we got information then we'd be in line for a reward maybe.'

'What makes you think it was stolen?'

I stared out of the window. Ian bit his finger. 'We had a look around.'

'You had no right.'

Ian shrugged.

'And you, Willie? You looked around too, did you?'

I nodded.

'I thought you had more sense.'

'Come on, Francis,' said Ian. 'Don't you think it's strange at all, a black fella coming in on a boat like that. And it's registered in Germany, did you know that?'

'You're a right mine of information, Ian Carey. But I have to tell you you're on the wrong track. Our lad is legitimate. It's not his boat, but he's skippering it back to Hamburg for the German owner.'

'Bikel Stengart,' I said.

'That's the one. So now you have it.'

'But if that Mr Stengart is just his owner why should he start crying when his name is mentioned?' I asked.

Francis raised an eyebrow. 'You'd have to ask him that yourself. But let the man be, do you hear me, boys?'

We nodded.

'I wouldn't want to hear of a couple of likely lads giving him bother.'

'Ach, come on, Francis . . . '

'You heard me.'

'Aye.'

'You can see yourselves out, lads.'

Seven

'We'll have to go back.'

'What?'

'On to *Katya.*'

'What?'

'The boat. Chrissakes, Willie, will you wake up!'

'You're off your head.'

We were sitting on the wall outside the shop, debating firstly whether we wanted an ice cream and secondly whether we had enough money to buy even one between us. At least that is what we had been debating all the walk back from Francis's house. Now we were just sitting.

Behind the sea breeze, the sun was warm on our faces and I was just happy to sit there and look out across Blacksod Bay to Kinfanalta Point on the far side and the mountains beyond. The sky was blue with a scattering of loose white cloud, and the sea was ruffled with short white-tipped waves—not rough, not inshore it wasn't, but out in the bay it would be, slopping about with seven, eight foot waves.

'Why'm I off me head?'

'The man had a knife and you were that frightened you passed out.'

'I did not.'

He kicked his heels against the wall and scowled. I smiled inside meself. Ian and I had never fought, which was a bit of a miracle considering how hot-tempered he is and how irritable I can be. And I'd been saving up to have a go at him for the way he'd had a fright last night.

We sat in a silence for a while. Then I said, 'Forget the

60

boat. That poor fella has enough troubles without the likes of us bothering him.'

The shop door tinkled and out came Anna. She greeted us friendly enough so I reckon either the African had told her nothing or she hadn't put two and two together, if you see what I mean.

Ian perked up instantly. 'Hey, Anna, when're you going to come out with Francis and me, out on his boat, fishing maybe.'

'Ian Carey, will you give it up. I am no more likely to go fishing than you are to become a millionaire. Or Willie here to turn into a poet of high repute.'

'I might,' I said.

She smiled. 'You might not. I tell you what, boys, if you win the curragh race I'll go dancing with ye afterwards.'

'That's cruel,' said Ian. 'You know Willie will never set foot in a boat.'

'Not even for me?'

I laughed. 'Well,' said I, 'miracles can happen, and then you'll be bound to keep your word.'

'I always keep my word.'

'Jayz, you're a flirt, Anna,' said Ian. He was only kind of jazzing her, but he didn't like her being friendly to me.

'How's your man, the African?' I asked. 'What do you call him anyhow?'

'His right name is Malouf, but the kids call him Malo,' she paused, glancing down the road from where we could hear a low rumble of powerful motors, not tractors, but cycles, big ones, you know. 'He's all right,' she said brightly. 'Still suffering from shock, I think.'

'Do you like him?'

She shrugged. 'Yes, he's nice. Different—' She broke off, distracted by the bikers. Like Vikings they were, five of them, two riding pillion, all with yellow hair and fancy mirror glasses and all of them on these massive silver and black machines. It would take your breath away, if you were impressed by that sort of thing. Ian was impressed, and so was Anna.

They pulled up right beside us, killed the motors, stretched and got off, talking loudly in a guttural sing-song, that sounded as strange to me as the black sailor. Two of them were birds. They'd knock you out to look at them, like in magazine pictures, legs as long as the Mullet itself, and gear you'd need to mend a mile of motorway to buy.

'Great looking bikes,' said Ian.

One of the men half turned. *'Ja,'* he said, casually over his shoulder. 'Up the IRA, yes?' and then turned back to his pals.

'Oh yes,' muttered Ian sarcastically, 'and the RTE.'

'And the UTV.' Probably been some lad in every village admiring their machines. Pissed me off though.

'CIA.'

'BMW.'

'Hitachi.' Ian did a loud cod sneeze that set us both laughing.

Anna told us not to be so rude because the one who had spoken to us glanced our way, but I think that was more because he had noticed Anna. Everyone always noticed Anna.

One of the girls strolled past us into the shop and then came out a few minutes later with a bunch of ice creams, and it all set them yo-hoing. I'm sure it was because the ice cream was only plain vanilla, and most likely out of date. Ours is not the greatest shop but it's the only one we have. I like Mrs Barratt and I suppose I don't like fancy tykes coming in thinking they're God Almighty, even if they are wearing black leather trousers.

'I must be off, boys,' said Anna.

'Sure.'

'I'd give anything for one of those bikes,' said Ian. 'I really would.'

One of the bikers touched Anna on the arm as she passed by. They were having some discussion over a map. 'Escuse me. You help? Which is Falmore road?'

Anna tossed back her hair, smiled, and fell into chat with the guy. 'I'll show you. It's no distance at all.'

There was more talk, and engines being started, one of the biker girls shrugging, I suppose she was being hooshed on to the back of another machine to make way for our Anna. A moment later the engines roared throatily and they pulled away one after the other. She didn't even look back. We might not have existed at all.

For a second I had one of those odd outside glimpses of ourselves—Ian, like his Aunt Brede, thin as a whippet, wiry arms and rough red hands; and beside him, in collar, tie, and blue jeans, a lanky lad with a young face and a shock of curly black hair. We didn't amount to much.

'Did you see that?' said Ian. 'I tell you, until we earn some real money, we're stuck, you and I.'

I ignored him but I knew what he meant. She might pass the time of day with the likes of us because she could hardly not, us having all known each other since we were toddlers, but you'd need to come riding by on a white stallion or a black BMW to win her heart. We watched them trail round the curve of the bay out towards Blacksod. On the side of the hill I could see a small, dark figure striding down, half running really, coming from the direction of the Macbraid house.

'Ah well,' I said, 'I think I'll be off too.'

'No, wait a minute.' His eyes were on the figure coming down towards the village as well. It was the African skipper, steaming along. 'I have an idea how to make a few bob.'

'Legally?'

'Reckon so.'

'Maybe we should wander off. See him later.' I thought that given what had happened last night he mightn't be best pleased to meet us again, right here in the middle of the village.

'What're you talking about? We didn't do anything, or break anything, or pinch anything. Just had a look around. Probably won't even recognize us.' And he folded his arms and whistled softly through his teeth.

Of course he recognized us. 'Hey!' he shouted when he was about twenty yards off. Ian pretended to ignore him but I kind of gave him a half wave.

'Hey!' To my surprise he seemed to be smiling. 'Two thief,' he said, jigging up and down on his toes. 'In my country phshweet . . . ' and he pretended to slit his throat with an imaginary knife. Grin as wide as Blacksod Bay. Having seen him taking a swipe with a real knife I didn't doubt that what he was saying was true, but he genuinely didn't seem to be that fierce about it. 'But then, boys, boys, always thief when they can.'

Ian in his most reasonable manner explained that we weren't by any stretch of the imagination thieves. Our African friend nodded and smiled but I'm not sure that he entirely understood. I was only grateful he didn't go shouting his head off. We would have looked a right pair, Ian and I, outside the shop with this fella telling all the world that we'd been snooping about on his boat at one o'clock in the morning.

Truth was, though, he wasn't actually very interested in us at all but wanted to know where Anna had gone. He thought he had seen her on the back of that fella's bike. When we confirmed that, and told him that the bikers were Germans he got positively edgy. I thought this sort of strange, and I wondered whether it had anything to do with the owner of his boat being German, but I couldn't figure out how.

'You admire our Anna, do you?' I said.

'Our?' That seemed to take him aback. 'She belong to you?' Ian laughed. 'I wish,' he said.

'It's just a manner of speaking,' I explained. 'A friend, that's all.' I felt like adding that people didn't belong like a piece of property, but I didn't like to say it in case that was the way it was back in his country.

'She is beautiful,' he said. 'She says she come to my country in my boat.'

'I think it is your boat that's beautiful,' said Ian. 'A real beauty.'

'Yes, fine boat.' He glanced in the direction that the bikers and Anna had gone, and then the opposite way, down the road to Elly. 'Where can I find bicycle?'

'A bike, sure, no bother. I'd say you want to be going out to your boat now, is that right?'

'Of course.'

'I'll come with you. Do you mind? I have some ideas, you know. To help.'

'You know about boats?'

'No man more,' said I. 'He has the sea in him. Ask Francis. You know Francis.'

'Oh yes. And you, other thief, you know boats?'

'William,' I said. 'That's my name.' And then, I don't know why, but I added, 'I can't stand the water at all.'

He looked at me narrowly. 'It makes you feel, here,' he thumped his chest, 'in your heart, fear, yes?'

I shrugged and looked away. 'I didn't say that, did I.'

'Yeah, but you are afraid, aren't you,' said Ian.

Isn't he the great pal. I expected this African skipper to show his white teeth and roar with laughter but to my surprise he put his hand on me shoulder, just like we were old pals, you know. 'One day you lose that fear,' he said.

'That's what I keep telling him,' said Ian.

The African held my eyes. It was kind of embarrassing for

I didn't know where to look, but the odd thing was I felt he was telling me something he knew, or at least he thought he knew. But how could anyone ever know what I would or wouldn't know? Hocus-pocus.

'Malouf,' he said, 'that is my name.'

'I know,' I said.

Well, that was it. We shook hands and he and Ian went off. I watched them trailing up the street together, Malouf not much taller than Ian and his hands going as he talked, waving them about, Ian's head turned half sideways, listening. Ian would borrow a couple of bikes without any bother.

I wondered how Malouf and he would get on, and what idea Ian had for making money. Because for all that Malouf was sailing a fine yacht, he didn't have the look of a man with buckets of cash. I think it was then that I realized that I liked him, and I think Ian probably did too, though it wouldn't get in the way of him earning his money. I wondered exactly how much Anna liked him.

There was a bit of a turn around when I got home. Mam had cooked a salmon for the Sunday dinner which was a big treat all right, and the girls were laying the table in the kitchen. Gary and Dad were sitting outside the back door, sheltered from the breeze and looking at the Sunday papers, while John James was loading his suitcases into his rented car. There was a silence about the place that you could chop in half with a spade.

I looked at Mary, and raised my eyebrows.

She wiped her hands down the front of her apron, 'Tell Dad and Gary to come in now,' she said to Jean, 'and John too.'

'Well?' I asked.

'Well nothing,' snapped my mother.

'It's hardly anything to do with Willie, Mum, is it?'

'If he hadn't made such a fuss about moving out of his room, then Johnnie wouldn't feel obliged to move out himself.'

'That's nonsense!'

I couldn't believe it. The two of them were spitting cross, and there was I, standing like an umpire watching the play. 'I made no fuss.'

'Your big brother,' said Mary, 'has decided to stay in the Royal Hotel in Belmullet, and Mum doesn't want him to go.'

'Oh,' I said. 'That's great.'

Now, in retrospect, that wasn't the wisest thing to say, but all I meant was that I would be pleased to sleep in my bed again, and I suppose if I were being honest I didn't much like having the big brother there anyway. Needless to say my mother saw red, and Mary, my lovely sister who had been taking my part, because Mum had already decided that it was all my fault that the big lump wanted to go, had to back down. Only John himself could pour oil on the troubled sea raging in the kitchen.

'It's nothing to do with William,' he said. He's the only one in the family who sometimes calls me by my full name. I think he does that because it makes him feel older and grander and not just my brother. 'I told you, ma,' a thin slice of his American accent slipping into the way he talked, 'I have this pal coming over and I reckoned it was better if we both stayed in town.'

'Sure, any friend of yours would be welcome here. Any number of neighbours would put him up.'

'I know,' said John, 'but he's only used to the city. I reckoned he'd be happier in town. And let's face it, it's a wee bit of a squash here right now, isn't it?'

'I don't think so.' She cut the salmon and served up.

'Let him go,' said Dad, speaking for the first time. 'It's his holiday.'

67

'That's right,' said John. 'I can be out every day, but it's handier for me, Mum. Brendan will want to play golf at Cross. And the truth is I want to try this new hotel. It might be a business opportunity. A little investment perhaps. You know I'm looking to put a bit of a stake into the community.'

'Like into Dracula,' I said.

Mary and Jean laughed. John ignored me.

'I'm also going to check out the island. Do you want to come, Dad, Mum, Gary, girls? I have asked Francis to take me out tomorrow afternoon if the day is fine enough. What do you say?'

This seemed to mollify my mother and there was energetic discussion about making the trip. Gary said it would be interesting, my mother said nothing in a million years would take her out to those wretched islands. My father said he didn't think he could, but wouldn't really explain why. Mary was working in town and Jean said that if Gary was going she would go too. She padded around after Gary like a proper collie, adoring him, and he was nice to her, except for the fact that he spent more time in the pub than anywhere else.

We had the meal, and me and the girls washed up. Then we saw John driving off in his fancy French car while Gary wandered down to the sea shore with Dad's old sea angling rod, Jean following him with a tin bucket for all the fish he was going to catch. Mum went up to Auntie Brede's and it just left Dad and myself. I asked him why he wouldn't go out to the islands with John.

'I have not been there since my wedding day, and I won't ever go back now.'

'Why is that?'

'It broke my heart to leave it once before.'

I always wanted him to tell me about the way they all left the islands, both communities, what was left of them, north and south. It must have been a sad time, a terrible sight. But he'd never talk about it. 'Why's John James wanting to go out?'

'John is always looking for ways to make money,' he said. 'And fair game to him.'

'Like Ian,' I said.

'No,' said my father, 'Ian is not like your brother John.' A moment later. 'Ian is all right.'

'I'd like to go out there, you know.'

'I know you would, lad. And it is fitting that you should. You have the island in you somewhere, more than the others.'

I looked at him when he said that, but he was just drawing on his pipe and looking out and away to the islands. He'd never said that before, never.

'But I'd have to cross the sea to get there.'

'You would,' he said.

'Well, I will do it, so. One time. I will.'

Eight

Most people round here have a few cattle. More bother than they're worth but it makes the family a few shillings and there's always the grant, so Dad says. It keeps him in beer anyhow. And it keeps me and Mary on the move, me mostly now, though Jeanie should be the one. But she's canny at skittering out of the way when there's jobs to be done.

We have a couple of fields behind the house; one that runs down to the shore on this side of the lane, and also grazing up the hill. Most evenings I bring the cattle in, so that we can milk them in the morning, and then the Co-op comes round and empties the two cans I leave up at the crossroads. And when I come back from school, I wash out the cans and bring the cattle back from wherever Mum has let them graze.

I suppose I don't mind. It's like brushing your teeth—you just do it. And on a day like this I could hardly complain. The sea, well you would have thought that Jesus himself had been taking a stroll along it, like he did in Galilee, it was that flat.

I walked up the hill to the tower. I had my fiddle with me, for though they say they don't mind me practising in the house, they do. There's always some programme on that they are wild about.

I'd been working on a tune that the band had played at Barratt's but every time I tried it it sounded sort of scraggy. I don't know what it is; I don't have a bad ear and I reckon I get my fingers in the right place but I just don't have it, not for rock and roll. 'Ye're not desperate enough,' that's what Ian says. Most of the musicians round this end of the

70

Mullet, the serious ones, the ones that can really play, aren't desperate at all. But they're all wedded to the pint, and that's my opinion.

Almost without thinking my fingers slipped into a jig. I played it a little slow, much like I do everything I suppose, and then with my eye half on the cattle I was supposed to be moving, I began to play odd notes, holding them longer and longer, and I heard the beginning of a tune, soft, an air you might call it. I didn't have it right, just the first glimpse of it, and then there was Ian, waving and yelling at me from down on the road.

I packed away and started on the cattle who came readily enough and then Ian and I drove them down to the house. He told me how he had done a few errands for the African skipper and had, in fact, changed his opinion of him altogether. 'He's all right, Willie,' he said. 'Not bad at all, and now I am a man with two salaries. What do you think of that?'

'I think you're a tinker.'

He ignored that and as we drove the cattle down, me with an eye on the white one that my dad calls Lady Scutter for she's forever cracking off sideways and causing a bother, he told me that our Malouf, with whom he seemed to have got mighty pally, was going to pay him to sleep out on the boat, like a security guard.

I was impressed, though Ian was not clear about how much he would actually get, which could only mean, to my way of thinking, that Malouf was maybe a cleverer talker than ever Ian was, but I said nothing on that.

'I'm out there tonight. Will you come out with me, Willie? It'll be a crack. Anna's coming down to the beach and we're going to cook something up on a fire, or at least himself is going to, probably just be sausages. Come on, bring the old fiddle.'

I said I wouldn't stay the night; my mother would flay me

if I wasn't in my own bed on the very night that John James was away in Belmullet and all because of me, according to her, that is. Sure, she had it fixed in her mind that I was the devil in the pot.

We settled the cattle in, picked up a few supplies from our fridge when no one was around, in case the African's food wasn't fit, as Ian put it, for human consumption, and then got the bikes and headed off.

Malouf was there at the beach when we arrived, and he already had a small fire going, a little ring of stones, and a smouldering heap of embers from driftwood, and a chicken roasting slowly over it. It looked mouthwatering to me.

'My thiefs,' he said, grinning like crazy and slapping us on the shoulders. 'Prepare yourself for magnificent food.' There was another pot simmering with a pinkish liquid bubbling quietly by his foot.

We offered the eggs and rashers we'd filched but he would have none of it and had us seated beside him cross-legged and with our plates balanced on our knees while he talked and cooked and served us up a meal like I'd never tasted before. Ian did a lot of face pulling but he is, after all, an idiot.

The clouds over the bay were wafer thin lines against a pale sky and the mountains way over on the mainland were dusky and as far away as a fairy tale. Anna drifted down and joined us, sitting down on the sand, but not eating, and not talking neither, but listening to him as he told us his story.

He was from a wee little village called Ideles, in the Sahara desert, high up near some mountains that are stuck there, right in the middle of nowhere, like the mountains of the moon. His village was seventy kilometres from the big highway, the route de Haggar, which he reckoned was mighty, and there would be a bus going on it most days, and lorries from time to time. And he travelled from there to the coast and then came all the way here on a boat. Travelling like that makes you wonder, doesn't it? It's not like the brothers getting on a plane and then getting off somewhere else. He crossed a desert of sand and then the ocean itself.

His village was what you'd call an oasis. 'Figs,' he said, 'we having many figs, and a well, and our houses white with flat roofs. Sleep under the stars. Very beautiful.' I could picture it all the way he talked; it was like a painting, and some of it was so different you would be lost and then other bits were just like home. They had telly and all. And they grazed, goats mainly, and sure they must have had a living but Malouf was not your usual cut of Arab-African or whatever, for though he wore the clothes, he was always looking for a way out of there, dreaming that he could be something different.

'Boys, you tell me,' he said, banging his hand against his knee. 'Why should I live my life in the dust, why? I can read, I have read many things. I have read your Shakespeare.'

Ian shook his head like he'd been whacked. 'Why the divil would anyone read that old stuff.'

'He's English, not Irish,' said Anna, watching him all the time, leaning forwards, her elbows on her knees, her chin cupped in her hands. 'I had to study *Othello* for the Leaving, you know.'

'Magnificent!' he exclaimed and then roared with laughter. 'Don't you think?' It was as if he hadn't heard either of them, he was that excited. 'I was not as other boys in my village. I was not.' He slapped his knee and swigged the beer that Anna had brought down—none for Ian or myself, mind you.

'Where'd you get the boat?' Ian asked.

'I will tell you how I, Malouf from Ideles, find a boat. Tourists,' he said, 'the life of my country is tourists. They come. They stay near the beaches but they come across the desert too. They come to the mountains of Haggar. They come to see women wearing chador, men in white. They come to see camels. They find us, they find heat, put your hand here, put it here, William thief, put it over the flame and tell me that does not hurt . . . ' Before I could move, he'd grabbed my wrist and pushed my hand over the flame, grinning while I yelled and tried to pull away.

It hurt, I can tell you. He laughed.

'This is nothing. There the road burns under your feet, and the sun burns your eyes. Yes.' He paused and gazed into the flame. 'Not many come to my part of my country and then come back again, not many. But there was one, who came and who came back and even found his way to my village. He was a German man, you know, Düsseldorf.'

And as he talked the stars began to come out and his yacht became a dark shadow on the glinting water of the bay. On nights like this I feel that the sky is made of blue-black velvet and it looks so soft you could bury your face in it. He told us that his father was the headman of his village but since he was the youngest in the family he had nothing to look forward to, maybe a few animals, scratching a life in the heat and the dust, maybe marriage for there were girls he had seen looking his way. But he wanted to be away, to follow the road towards the big towns, the way many from his village had done before.

Then something happened that changed his life, he said. A tour bus pulled into the village. This sometimes happened, especially on market day when men would come down from the mountain villages to trade and the tourists would take photographs and perhaps drink tea and then would be gone.

This time though it was different. Malouf was there, sitting at the door of his parents' house, idle. He watched the silver bus with its black-tinted windows—'So they could see us and we not see them'—pull into the little square and then stop. Its engine was humming softly. There were many stalls, and a camel trader was doing business. No one minded the bus, except perhaps Malouf who had little to do but watch.

After a little while the door opened and two people came out, both elderly. A couple; she in a straw hat and a fancy looking black leather bag over her shoulder; he in a white suit and with a cane, though he walked well enough, Malouf thought. Rich, they were certainly rich by his standards.

No one else got out, and the door shut. Malouf stood up and came closer, not crowding, just keeping an eye on them for there was always the chance of earning a little money.

He figured they were Germans, which was a pity for he only had a few words of German at that time. He could hear the man talking to a stall-holder who could not understand him. Then the tourist changed to English and Malouf stepped in. They were happy for him to translate but then when they fell to talking he could see that they were different in some way from those Europeans who came holidaying in what to them were strange lands. The man was not well. When Malouf got close to his face he could see that it was hollowed out with his sickness and there was a rasp and rattle in his breath that was not good, Malouf could tell that. The lady it turned out was a friend, not his wife, and she was not so content as he was to wander through Ideles.

When the coach sounded its horn, and Malouf made to lead them back to the square, the man restrained him and said he wished to stay on, and could Malouf find them a car to rent. Malouf was able to do anything they wanted as long as there was money. At that stage that was all he was interested in.

The lady grew impatient. There were angry words in German and Malouf took her back to the bus. As she got on to the step, she turned and looked him in the face, looking into him, so that he had to turn his eyes away, and she made him promise to look after the man. He did, a solemn oath, and then the door slid closed and the bus pulled away and that was the last he ever saw of her. He hurried back to his German tourist.

'I look after him as if he is my father. I take him everywhere he want to go. My home is his home, but we do not stay in Ideles long. We have car, Mercedes, and we drive to the mountains, to Anhaggar, to the big cities of my country. We go everywhere, everywhere.' He laughed and his eyes and teeth flashed in the firelight. 'You drive Mercedes?'

'I believe they are beautiful on the inside,' says Anna.

I couldn't help thinking that was a sort of daft thing to say, but she wasn't listening to herself, I could tell that. She was breathing in his story like the sweet smell of this salty beach fire.

'They're good cars all right. Great motor,' said Ian. 'You see tourists with them sometimes, you know.' He crossed his legs and leaned forward. 'Is he the fella then that gave you the boat . . . ?'

'Good leather, fine engine . . . ' Malouf closed his eyes and took a long deep sniff, pulling up his shoulders as he did so. 'I love that car, but not,' he says all dramatical, 'because of these things but because I am free.'

'Except for your man, the tourist,' says Ian drily.

'Ah no, he is no more the tourist, my Irish thief. He is my new father. I keep him always safe. I keep him from bad men.'

'What bad men is that?'

He hesitated and then shrugged. 'There is always bad men, but not like here where all are kind to Malouf, eh, except a little bit of thief. More wood, more wood for the fire, come,' and he jumped up and with Ian walked briskly along the edge of the sand and shingle to where we had spotted driftwood earlier. Anna and I got up more slowly.

'Why's he keep saying that "my thief" business, Willie? Did the two of ye do something?'

'Ah, not really.' And I told her how we had gone out to the boat and he had found us there. In fact I thought she would have known already for he didn't seem to me to be the sort of man to hold much back. He was so open, or seemed so, that you could imagine him confiding his life story to the first person he met in the village shop.

But when I told her this, Anna laughed and said that he talked all right but he'd made no mention of us at all. 'Ian's a right messer, isn't he?' she said.

'I was out there too.'

'You mean you had to paddle all the way out there, getting yourself all wet?'

'So?' I'm not crazy about being teased.

Her voice softened a little. 'You hate that, don't you, Willie?'

'It's no great secret.'

'Would you rescue me if I were drowning?' There was a funny, half serious note to her voice and I didn't quite know how to reply.

Then the others were back and she was looking up and smiling at Malouf, who with Ian tossed a good-sized slab of driftwood on to the fire. For a while we talked about nothing much at all, just this and that and enjoying the warmth of the flame and the crackle and spit of the fire.

'But how did you get your boat?' asked Ian again. 'Because, Jesus, for something like that to land in your lap is like winning the lotto, you know.'

'But it was him, of course,' said Malouf, as if surprised by the question, 'my German father. He has the boat, crew, everything. He is rich man. I tell you this, he teach me to sail, everything . . . ' His voice trailed off into silence for a moment, 'so that when he die I can sail it home for him, back to Germany.' He clapped his hands. 'And this is what I do. See. He gave it me, this boat. He gave me . . . new life. All I must do is take *Katya* to Germany and there I have boat, house, everything. I am rich man now, Anna. I tell you all this. I may have small little shipwreck but I am rich man, not in my country but the one to which I go. There I am rich.'

He bubbled and laughed as he said this to us and we couldn't all help grinning and laughing along with him.

I played a jig and he and Anna danced, well, after a fashion that is. She'd kicked off her shoes and danced neatly enough. He watched for a moment and then stalked around her, arms stretched out, doing his own footwork like nothing I had ever seen before. And all the time his arms out, like wings, steady. It was a great sight the two of them, shadowy on the edge of the firelight.

Ian was sitting beside me, beating time with his hands on his legs. 'Pity the godstone is lost,' he said. 'I'm thinking that this man could do with powerful blessing to get himself home.'

'You don't believe that stuff, do you?' I said.

'Your old fella does, Willie. Don't you?'

I thought about it, while the two danced, and the log sputtered on the fire. 'Maybe.'

Anna dropped down on to the sand beside me, Malouf stood behind her. 'What're you both so serious about?'

'Just talking,' I said.

'About the godstone, you know,' said Ian.

'Ach, that old thing . . . '

But Malouf wanted to know all about it, so Ian told him about our little bit of magic, I mean the godstone. And how it helped to keep the fishermen safe, them that took it serious, that is. Nobody knows where it came from, but it was there, kept in the little church for hundreds of years,

78

ever since priests had been coming out to the islands. They knew better than to meddle with it, and would just shake a bit of holy water on it at Christmas and saints' days.

But then there was one notorious father who fell into the parish. O'Reilly was his name and he would have none of the godstone. He went at the island men and the women and roared at them that it was pagan and unholy and he got the bishop to order the men of the islands to get rid of it. And so they did. They took it to the deep channel, where the whole of the Atlantic pours between the north and south island and they pitched it in. As far as anyone knows that's where it lies to this day.

That's what Ian related that night.

'Did it have real power?' asked Malouf.

'I'll tell you this,' said Ian. 'Thirty years after they lost it to the ocean, there wasn't a sinner left on the islands.'

'That was good then?'

'No,' said Anna, 'he means they all left. There was a fierce storm. The young men were drowned, and within a couple of years the islanders came over to here.'

'Ah,' he sighed. 'Their hope was gone.'

Without really thinking I had begun to play the beginning of the air that I had been fiddling at that morning, just softly.

'That music. It's like the quiet sea,' said Ian, 'slow dancing.'

Funny. You wouldn't have thought someone like Ian could come up with something like that; but he was right. There was that kind of breathing waltz that the sea, even at its quietest, still has.

'Sad,' said Anna.

Aye, it was that too. I hadn't meant it to be, but that's the way it happens at times.

She got up and Malouf took her hand and they walked a little ways down the beach. The two of us stayed sitting, me playing the while, both of us watching, knowing as you do when you're maybe not so welcome. And our Anna and that African man looked awful still together, one shadow almost. I think she was showing him how to dance, slowly you know, there on the strand, with the water of the bay darkly glinting behind them.

Then behind my music I heard a car approaching. I remarked it for there hadn't been any in a long while and mostly you wouldn't notice because they would be passing by quickly, for there was nothing here to stop for, not at this time of night. But the car was coming slowly. Perhaps the driver was drunk and feeling his way home, sticking well to the middle of the road. I could see the lights now and as the road curved towards the beach, slowly they raked the length of the strand like a man with a torch looking for something he'd lost.

'What are they at?' muttered Ian.

I stopped playing.

Whoever it was behind the wheel was no drunk.

The lights slid slowly over the strand, coming closer all the time, and then they picked out Malouf and Anna. They were dancing, oblivious, hands on each other's shoulders, caught in the light. I saw Malouf blink and shake his head, and tighten his arms around her and she with her back to the light all the time.

The headlights held them for a moment, and then the car's engine revved and the car swung away sharply and drove off.

'Who was that?' said Ian.

I shook my head. All I knew was that it wasn't nice, not at all. Like staring and picking a fight, somehow, and no voice, no name you could put to it, and you couldn't even see the car. 'Some bowser,' I said, packing away my fiddle.

'Do you want to stay on the boat?'

'Are you kidding?' Then I glanced towards Malouf and

80

Anna, they were walking slowly away from us. 'You don't think he'll be wanting the boat . . . '

'No.' Then a moment later. 'I wouldn't say so. Anyhow I'm off, see you tomorrow.' With that he walked down to the edge of the shore and I heard the sliding scrunch of the rubber dinghy he was using being hauled down into the water and the slip and drip of his paddle.

I would have liked to have said something to Malouf about the car and all, but I didn't want to shout, and I didn't want to run after them. I didn't know what I could say except to tell him to watch himself, so instead I turned and walked up to where I had left my bicycle.

Away from the fire, the night was cool on my cheeks.

Nine

There, about ten feet below me, was a crab about the size of my hand, scuttling in and out of the weed, swashing to and fro with the incoming tide. Like a dance, out on to the sandy floor, claws waving, then sideways for a foot or so, and then back again.

'Were you ever on the island, Willie?'

I started. The question coming so close to my thoughts, I felt, I don't know, transparent somehow. I shifted round and looked up at the lanky figure of Francis, squinting, for though it was early, the sun was up and bright. He had the dark glasses on; he was a fair cool character, Francis. 'No,' I said and looked back down again, but my crab had gone to wherever crabs go when they're not dancing to the tune of the tide.

'You know John James is going out this morning.'

I was on the edge of the quay at Blacksod, my legs dangling over the side, just watching the tide come in, seeing the water lick around the grounded hull of an open-decked fishing boat called the *Marie*, and thinking about a whole scad of things. Trying to get some order into it all and not managing because I could never concentrate for more than a second before I'd switch to the next thing: there was our African and what would happen to him and his boat; and would Anna be leaving the Mullet to go away with him when he went; and I was thinking about what one or two people were saying about him and her, and wondering if there would be trouble. I hadn't liked the way that car had stopped and caught them in the headlights.

I was also wondering about my brothers: how long they'd

stay, and I was speculating about this Yank friend of John James's whom I hadn't even seen yet. What would he be bringing a Yank back home for when a fool could see he didn't give a spit for the old place.

And, most of all, as I was staring down into that crystal water I was thinking about the sea and the islands that were so far beyond my reach. That was the spot Francis's words had touched, a sore spot and all.

'I know,' I said. That's why I was there, of course, to watch them setting off. Tight as a clam my brother was, wouldn't say a thing about why he was going out to the islands. He and his fancy friend had spent the last three days driving all round the coast of Mayo, checking this and checking that and not once coming out to the house.

My mother wasn't at all happy. Nor was I. What did he want out there at all? I swallowed back the bitterness that was making my mouth sour and glanced at Francis.

'How long before you can set off?' I asked.

Francis's boat, a thirty footer he used for trips to the islands and for taking out sea anglers, was moored out from the shore; his tender, a curragh, was hauled up on the beach.

He squatted down beside me and lit a cigarette. 'About twenty minutes and I can bring her in. It should be a good day.' We lapsed into companionable silence. Then he said, 'It's not like John James to be wanting to go out to the islands, is it?'

I shrugged.

'Maybe he's wanting to show them off to his friend.'

'I hope you're charging him the full rate,' I said.

'A man has to live. You know Ian's coming with me?'

I nodded. 'He's still out on the African's boat, minding it.'

'I heard that.' He flicked his cigarette out into the water and stood up. 'The place is fairly crawling with strangers this summer. I hope that brother of yours hasn't too many smart ideas. I remember him at school; he was always the one with smart ideas and they usually ended in someone getting hurt. Give us a hand launching the curragh, will you?'

We walked back along the quay and then jumped down the couple of feet on to the sand. You wouldn't think curraghs are heavy but, by God, they are, if they're made from wood and not canvas, and this one was wooden. Francis liked things to be solid and sure. We sweated at it and shifted it down the couple of yards to the water. Then, he on one side and me on the other, we hauled it out. I hesitated just for a fraction, then kicked off my runners and waded out. The sand was warm but the water was cold. The water is always cold round here. Francis jumped in and unshipped the oars while I held on to the gunwale.

'Is there any truth in all that business of the godstone, Francis?'

His eyes were blank to me behind the dark glasses. I wondered whether there was a hint of a smile there, but you couldn't tell at all. 'Who knows,' he said. 'But it's not the sort of thing you would want to talk to your brother and his Yankee friend about, is it?'

'Why not?' Not that I ever would.

'Ah, you know, he'd be starting tours and selling chips to the tourists before you could say cash profit. Is that what you'd want?'

'Who would?'

'There'd be some. Your brother for one.' He braced himself against the middle thwart. 'Give her a good shove.'

I did and Francis leaned on one of the long oars and poled himself out a few yards. 'Come out with me one time, Willie, and I'll show you a couple of things out there that would interest you.'

I lifted my hand and he gave a brief nod and then hooked in the other oar, and rowed standing, the way all the older fishermen used to do.

I went back up on to the quay. The *Marie* had begun to float, and the water was no longer so clear; her keel was scuffling up the sand I suppose. A battered green Ford drove up and Jimmy Byrne and his dad got out and we exchanged greetings. 'Are you coming out with us today, Willie?'

'Another day maybe.'

Jimmy laughed.

'Grand day,' said his father.

'It is, thank God.'

When Ian rolled up I asked him what he was doing going out on a trip with my brother, but for Ian cash was always a major incentive and he said he reckoned he could put up with John James so long as he didn't have to talk with him. I said I reckoned that sleeping out on that grounded yacht, all keeled over the way it was, was making him soft in the head. He laughed and told me how Malouf was not only promising him good money but, and this was what really had him excited, he'd said he could crew with him out to Germany, and that out there maybe he could set him up with work.

'For Chrissakes, Ian, you've another year of school yet. Brede will chew you to bits if you talk about setting off. I told you you were cracked.'

He grinned. 'She'll be delighted to see me go. Jesus, Willie, it's my real chance. I might not get another as good as this. Can you imagine, I could be back in a year and like that swanky brother of yours have money in my pocket.'

'And Anna would fall in love with you and you'd ride off into the sunset. You're daft!'

'I am not. I'll make something of meself, Willie, and if you had any sense you'd come with me. Why don't you?'

I'd not seen him in this good form for a long while, if ever, come to think of it. Practically every sentence began with 'That Malouf . . . '; you'd think he was Father Christmas the way he was going to make everything right.

Me, I hadn't seen the African skipper since that night on the beach and that was almost a week, for I'd been busy with the hay, and helping out around the headland.

And there was a dance coming up too, at Barratt's again, a local band from Belmullet were playing. I knew the drummer and he'd asked if I'd be willing to sit in for part of the set, so I'd been practising like crazy.

The tide was well in now and we watched the *Marie* cast off and nose her way out from the quay and then Francis's boat coming in to take her place. God, it was a fine day. I swore then that I had to learn to sail on the water or I'd be haunted all my life. I would do it . . . I would do it.

'Here come the Yanks.'

John's car roared up, far too fast, braked with a squeal, kicking up the dirt over us and then out John sprang. 'How're you, lads? Francis, hey, are we ready to go?'

'No hurry.'

Ian took the line Francis had thrown him and looped it round a bollard while Francis climbed up on to the quay to meet John and the American, and, to my surprise, Anna who'd been sitting in the back of the car. Maybe they'd given her a lift; maybe she was going out with them. I hoped not. I wondered what our Malouf would say.

Ian scowled. 'What's she doing with them?' he muttered.

'Maybe she hasn't heard your plans yet.' He didn't smile.

The American was, in his own way I suppose, a good looking man. Same age as John, but slighter and as dapper as a dummy from a shop window, wearing all the right clothes but with neat creases in them, you know. He had a suede shoulder-bag that looked as if it might contain half the contents of a Dublin camera shop.

I stood up—it'd be only courtesy to say hello—and heard him saying to Anna, 'Are you sure you won't come with us, honey . . . '

Honey! I nearly died. I thought Yanks only said that on telly.

'No thanks,' she said.

'Well, see you when we get back.'

She smiled, and pushed the hair back out of her eyes.

'Yeah, see you,' said John and then to me: 'All right, William?' and gave me a nod.

'Ye've chosen a great day. Is this your friend?'

The Yank looked right through me and then putting his hand on John James's shoulder talked to him earnestly. You know: mutter mutter with John nodding like a funny man. I think the pair would have walked right over me if I hadn't backed out of the way.

When they reached the edge, the Yank stood looking down on to Francis's boat for a moment.

'Will she do you?' said Francis blandly.

'What? Oh, the boat. Why, sure. Of course it's not that far out to these islands, is it?'

'No distance at all,' said Francis.

John slapped his pal on the shoulder and the two of them scrambled down.

Ian raised his eyebrows. 'Great company,' I said to him.

'No kidding.'

'Let us go there, Willie,' called Francis from the wheelhouse.

I unlooped the rope from the bollard and dropped it down to Ian.

I didn't take to that Yank. People who don't see you when you're right in front of them, and it's your place anyhow, people like that are cold to the bone.

Anna came up and stood beside me and the two of us watched the little boat pull around the quay and then surge off out towards the point before cutting to the channel between Duvillaun and Falmore and then out to sea.

'How're you, Willie?'

'I'm grand,' I said flatly, 'but I don't think much of the company you're keeping.'

'Is that right?' She smiled and took my arm. 'Are you jealous?'

'I am not,' I said. 'Not even you could be daft enough to see anything of value in my brother.'

She paused. 'I don't know,' she said. 'He's a big head, I suppose, but that's not always so terrible, and he dresses well, for a man.'

'And his pal?'

She laughed. 'He's rich.'

We walked back down the quay together and when we'd got to where Francis and I had jumped down on to the sand I said, 'You know you were joking about me and Ian rowing in the curragh race?'

'Yes.' She was turned to face me and the bit of breeze was lifting her hair and tugging it and her eyes were crinkled up a little because of the sun, and maybe because of that smile of hers I found myself saying, 'Teach me to row, Anna.'

'What do you mean?'

'Teach me. Right here. Just in this quiet bit of water. I want to learn . . . '

'Just to row, so that you can go in a race. Are you cracked? I was only codding you the other day. You don't think I'd marry the either of you in a million years.' There was a hint of annoyance in her voice that hadn't been there a moment before.

'No, I don't think that.' Million years. Millionaires. 'I'm not stupid, and it's not winning the race that bothers me.'

It wasn't the race at all, but the sea itself I needed to beat. I think I'd just seen a boat setting off across the blue one too many times.

Her smile seemed to soften a fraction. After a second she shrugged. 'Sure,' she said. 'Why not.'

Well, I can tell you that you do not want to know about my

rowing except that I didn't panic or throw up but I sweated so much I thought I'd drown without even putting my foot in the water. I was pleased enough I had got through it, though we didn't go out more'n twenty yards I'd say, and all that time I fixed my eyes on Anna.

'Willie! Will you stop staring at me. You look frightening.'

I tried to smile but she said that was worse; it made me look like a serial killer.

I asked her if she was going to marry the African. Ian called him Mali now and said he was a crack. I thought Ian pushed it a little bit, you know, treating him almost like Malouf were the kid brother or a touch simple. I didn't think he was at all. I couldn't call him Mali and somehow to Anna I couldn't even use his right name. Don't ask me why.

'Are you crazy?' she said. Her eyes were squinted against the sun, and there was a tiny bead of sweat on her upper lip that she wiped away with her wrist. 'Pull on that oar. No, the right one, you daft eejit, and bring us in.'

'Will you come out with me again?' I said when we had hauled the dinghy up the beach. 'You know, when maybe there aren't that many people around.'

She laughed and then touched my arm. 'Maybe. I hear you're playing at the dance on Saturday.'

'Aye.'

'That'll be great.' Her eyes rested on my bike. 'Is that your bike? I couldn't borrow it ever, could I? I'm in a terrible race.'

'Of course.'

I watched her set off. The seat was too high for her and her backside wobbled, and although I didn't really want to walk all the way back to Aghleam and then back home, because it would take me a good three quarters of an hour, I can't say I was angry with her. She looked funny anyhow.

I saw Malouf outside the post office when I finally drifted

into the village. He was just stepping out of the phone box and his face was like he'd just received the most terrible news, crushed, you know. And then he saw me and he was suddenly all wreathed in smiles.

'Willie!' he shouted at me and waved and I went over and chatted for a minute. Everything was wondrous, he said, everything was fine. His money order was coming through. Work would start on *Katya* next week. He and Ian would sail for Germany . . . and then like a hare he was loping off up the hill to the Macbraid house. He never once asked me about anything. I thought he was odd at the best of times, but he was getting odder by the minute if you asked me.

I went into the shop and there was Mrs B and Annie Dean hooped over the counter having a fierce conversation together and I could hear them hissing about 'the darkie' so it didn't take a genius to know they were discussing Malouf. I asked for an ice cream and because I knew she'd have been listening in to his conversation as she listened in to most people's, I couldn't help saying, 'He was phoning Germany, I suppose, was he?'

'Germany, begod, is it. Two hours I had to set up that telephone communication for him. Africa was who he was talking to.'

'Is that right, Mrs B, and who was he talking to there?'

'Well I don't know, do I? I don't speak African, you stupid child . . . but whoever it was he was shouting his head off out there, and,' she said underlining the word in case I would miss the significance of whatever it was she was going to tell me, 'they put the phone down on him.'

I don't know what mile of gossip she would get out of that but I have to say I found it puzzling. No, maybe not puzzling.

Was he a fake?

Ten

Aunt Brede has three good long fields of hay that stretch out from behind her house to back along the cliff edge. Ted Moran had cut them a week back and, given that we'd had a couple of good dry days, it was no surprise that Gary was all for getting it cocked.

I arrived back at Glosh after picking up my bike from the Macbraid household; she'd left it at the gate so I didn't bother to go in but I'd heard laughing and seen her little brothers, Mick and Dolan, scattering about and Malouf roaring after them like the divil from the deep, and Anna at the doorway watching and laughing. It was a good sight.

Gary was waiting for me. 'Isn't Ian the lucky one,' he said handing me one of the hay rakes, 'lazing away on that boat.'

'And John.'

'You don't think he'd rough his soft hands up on a rake do you?' said Gary spitting into the palms of his hands and rubbing them together. 'He's other plans altogether.'

'Oh?' I was curious to know his plans all right. 'What are they?'

'His plans? Ach, he would never tell me anything, but I'd say he has them, you can be sure of that, and each one of them will make him a bucket of money.'

'What's he doing going out to the islands, Gary?'

'Just being the tourist with his Yank friend.'

'Nothing more?'

'What more is there? They're just lumps of rock out in the Atlantic, and not a drink to be had on the pair of them.'

We strolled over the lane to the fields. It was such a clear day you could see the islands as if they were a photograph: the grey ruined houses round the harbour, the stone walls narrowing up the one hill to the monument at the top. I could see Francis's boat all right; he'd pulled out from the harbour and was motoring slowly along the shore of north island, doing a spot of fishing probably, unless John had wanted him to take them on to the north island as well. He might have done.

It's a long business working at a field and there is no point in rushing it. You work steady. Sometimes you might work together and sometimes you'd work on your own. Gary and I worked separate, raking and stooking and moving down the field, he on the one side and me on the other. After an hour the sweat was pouring off us both, and bits of hay were sticking to my neck and catching in my throat.

'Time she bailed it up for silage,' grunted Gary.

'She'd never do that. She hates the black plastic.' I hated it too. I hated the shiny round black lumps in the cut fields; and I hated the shreds of long wet plastic, strung out on the wire, or washed up on the beaches when the silage was gone.

'Maybe she's right,' said Gary, 'but it makes an easier job.' He threw down his rake and went over to the house to get us something to drink and I dropped down on the shady side of one of the haycocks and took my ease.

They say you should never fall asleep in the full day sun for the fairies may come and take your soul. Well, I must have been more tired than I reckoned and Gary a lot longer than he said, for I did doze off, and I was straight into that dream. Every night, now, every night it came to me. Cool green water, like a wall rising up above me and the white arms reaching out through the wall to me, either for my help, so that I could heave them out, or to pull me in, I could never tell. All I knew was the fear that made me look and didn't let me leave. And that wasn't the worst of it.

I awoke with a start.

'Only a thief and a wise man sleeps when the village works. This is what they say in my home.' Malouf was standing with a wide smile on his dark face. 'What are you, Willie? A thief I think.'

'Not a lot to steal out in this field,' I said. 'What are you doing here?'

'Your brother said . . . you'd not mind if I offered a hand.' He spoke carefully, no doubt trying to catch what Gary had actually said.

I laughed. 'He's right. I wouldn't mind at all.'

Gary came up behind him carrying another hay fork, and a couple of bottles of water, which he and I drank in small sups but which Malouf declined. They don't have much water where he comes from. We worked on until the late afternoon, completing the first and then the second field. 'He's all right, your man,' said Gary taking a break with me, and leaning on his fork, watching Malouf piking up a swathe of hay and coiling it into the cock.

'He learns quick enough,' I said.

'They were saying down in the pub that he's cracked, not all there, you know.'

I shrugged. 'He's in good enough company in this village then.'

'That's true.' He smiled. 'It'll not rain tonight. What do you say we finish this tomorrow? Brede'll not mind.'

'Suits me.'

At that moment Malouf shouted to get our attention and waved towards the sea. There was Francis's boat already halfway back from the islands.

'I'm off,' said Gary. 'Do you and your pal fancy a drink later?'

'Maybe.'

I watched Gary walking up the field, stopping to pass a word to Malouf, nodding back towards me, then striding off again. A whole long day out in the sun, making the hay, and he still walked with a bounce in his stride. He was fierce strong, Gary, and he loved his pint. Just the thought of it was enough to make him happy.

Me, I was half dead, my hands were raw and the back of my neck was roasting from the sun. I let my rake drop and picked up the bottle of water. It was getting on the warm side, but I took a sup anyhow and then ran it into my hands and sloshed it over my face.

'Your islands?' said Malouf coming up beside me.

I offered him the bottle. He took it and poured a tiny drop into the pink palm of his dark hand and touched it to his lips.

'Aye, they're my islands,' I replied. 'Not that I've ever been to them, but I'll go there yet.'

'Why will you? They have nothing, or do they?'

I thought about this for a moment. No they didn't have anything, not for someone whose only interest was for going to a rich country like Germany and starting up a new life, but for me they had something.

'My father was born there,' I said. 'And his father before him . . . ' I shrugged.

'Perhaps you want to find the holy stone?'

I'd forgotten we'd even told him about that. Funny what some people remember. 'I don't know about that.'

'From Ideles,' he said, 'I can see the mountains. They look like a dream, like your islands. And they call to us, the mountains, but there is nothing there, only stone and dangerous paths.' He dusted a fly from his face.

'Will you go back?'

'Why go back? Never go back, Willie. The past is full of shadows; the future full of light.'

I smiled. 'That's a nice enough way of putting it. You're a right optimist, Malouf.'

He shrugged. 'I am thousands of miles from my home, a

thousand miles from the end of my journey, my boat is broken and look at me, making hay in Ireland, and a very happy man.'

'Oh?'

'Anna will marry me.'

'Will she?'

'Of course.'

Not much you can say to that. We picked up the forks and headed back to Brede's. I didn't mention what Anna had said to me. It hardly seemed kind. And I also said nothing about that phone call he'd made, though I was dying to ask what all the shouting had been about. Still it was none of my affair.

Brede let us wash and then gave us tea and didn't blink when Malouf asked to drink his out of a little whiskey glass, and with no milk or sugar in it at all. She was courtesy itself, which is more than can be said for my mother who called in to take a look at the African himself. She kept well over by the door, as if maybe he would leap at her or something, and she avoided shaking his hand which mortified me. Thank God she didn't stay long.

'I'd say you're getting used to our odd ways by now,' said Brede to him.

'Ah no. Not so odd. People are the same. Underneath we are the same.'

'True enough,' said Brede, 'though there'd be a few around here that wouldn't agree with you.'

I was surprised to hear her say that for I always reckoned that folk at our end of the Mullet were the warmest and friendliest folk in the world, or at least I presumed they were. Sure, everyone said it about the Irish anyway. But then I remembered the way they had talked about Malouf in the shop, and I began to wonder.

By the time we were ready to leave Brede's it was too late to make our way over to Blacksod and see the boat coming in, so we strolled up the lane, cutting across the edge of Termon Hill till we were above Aghleam, and then down the hill to Barratt's.

Gary was up at the bar and waved us over. He insisted on buying a round, and wouldn't hear of Malouf having anything other than a pint of Guinness. I thought it was against his religion to drink alcohol but he took the pint all the same and drank it. I had a Coke.

Ian came in after about half an hour, bobbing up and down like a maniac he was so full of good news. 'I'm a rich man,' says he. 'No more lottery tickets for the likes of me.'

'Tell us your secret,' says I.

'Don't tell me you don't know what John James is up to?'

Gary and I looked at each other.

'No.'

'You have land up on the island, don't you, Willie?'

'I suppose so. Well it is Dad's really, though I think he has already put it in our names. At least I have a feeling that was what he did when he went to see the solicitor in town.'

'Just make sure that it is in your name, that's all,' said Ian, 'otherwise John James will lay claim to the lot.'

'He's welcome to it,' said Gary. 'Who would want to be stuck out there with nothing but seagulls yelling at you all of the day.'

'Well, he's promised to buy my land from me,' said Ian. 'I am worth two grand. Two grand! Think of it. I'm set up now, Willie.'

I couldn't believe it somehow, it was like selling your birthright. Sell the islands and then there was no going back. Maybe Ian was more like Malouf than I had ever thought. Ah no, it shouldn't have surprised me. He could never see further than the nearest prospect of a pound note.

'More fool you,' I said. 'I bet that was a bad price he gave you.'

'Don't be daft! What's a bad price for one poor field and a single-room house with no roof to it.'

I said nothing.

'Two thousand pounds. That'll help set me up in Germany won't it, Mali?'

'Very good,' said Malouf. 'It's a wise man who carries little on his shoulder.' He stood up and offered to buy us all drinks.

I followed him over to the bar. It wasn't Mick serving but one of his helpers, a fella from the next village. He pulled a pint readily enough, and got us a bag of crisps and Coke for Ian. I didn't want anything.

'I will pay later,' said Malouf and picked up the glasses to carry them across to the table.

I have to say I thought it was a bit strange, but not as strange as the lad behind the bar who said, 'You'll pay now or you can get out as far as I am concerned, darkie.'

Malouf, the picture of indignation now, straightened himself up and eyed the lad like he were total gobshite from the gutter. 'I know Barratt,' he said haughtily. 'It will be all right. I am not offended by you.'

And he turned to go.

'Is that right?' said the lad loud enough for all in the bar to hear. Malouf stopped. 'Offended or not, ye can take a walk for all I care. Now pay up or get out.'

'Here,' I said. I had a handful of change in my pocket which I slapped on the counter.

'Suits me.' The lad slid the money into the till and gave me the change. 'But you can tell your black friend that there's no credit for him here.'

'Since when are you laying down the law in Mick's place?' I said. I was cross enough, I can tell you. All the money I had was in my pocket and while I didn't like the way this tyke was talking, I was equally annoyed by Malouf being so high and mighty.

'Since he told me not to let anyone have credit, and if you don't like it you can have it out with Mick yourself.'

I went back to the table and said nothing about it. And I didn't even push Malouf to see me right over the couple of quid, but I didn't forget it either and it set me thinking, and worrying too. It was three weeks since Malouf had been blown in on the storm and in that time there had been an awful lot of talk but no sign of anything happening to his boat. Surely he must have had some money with him, or a way of getting cash. You couldn't set off on a journey like from Africa to Germany without a way of buying yourself food, that was too stupid.

I bumped into Francis the next day and asked him about the trip and how he'd liked the Yank. He pulled a face. 'Fair weather sailor,' he said and spat. 'Was only interested in the stone Jesus. Tried to make me believe it ought to be in a museum and that he knew someone who knew someone who would take it off our hands and it might be worth a few pounds.'

The stone Jesus is up there on the north island by the remains of an old monastic hut. Very old, maybe over a thousand years Francis says, for that's what a scholar told him one time. Hard to believe the islands were inhabited that long ago, and had monks there and all, but they did. Must have been hardy men.

'What did you say to him?' I asked.

'I said that it belonged on the island and not in a museum. I think he got the message.'

I then asked him if there was any word on Malouf's boat but he had heard nothing either. 'He'll need to make a start because the summer won't last for ever,' he said.

I am sure he was right but the next few days turned into a week and the summer was finer than I can ever remember,

98

blue skies and warm sun, and the sea soft and calm. Ian still stayed out on the boat at night but had started to grumble that it was about time he got sight of some money.

John James and his American friend disappeared into town and rarely came out to us at all, but I heard that he had visited most of the old island families and had bought up a fair number of ruined houses on the south island, but not much land. People are funny about selling fields, people apart from Ian that is.

I didn't like it, but what could I do. He had the money and why should I stop him owning some place I couldn't even get to. But it hurt somehow. I didn't say anything to anyone, least of all Ian.

Anna took me out in the curragh again and I managed a little better. Well, at least I didn't panic and I reckon I got the knack of pulling the oars without falling off my seat. It wasn't rowing that was a problem, I must have had that skill in my blood, it was just knowing that you were sitting up above water, and the green darkness was all below you. I concentrated on her and I tell you that helped mightily.

I hadn't seen Malouf for a couple of days, not since that business in the pub in fact, and I asked her about him. She shrugged. 'I've no idea about him at all.'

That didn't sound right to me and I said as much. After all, he was staying at her house.

'Mam isn't happy,' she said eventually. 'It's not that it's that expensive keeping him, and I suppose he does help out, but it's another mouth to feed, that's what she keeps saying.'

'Don't you think he'll be getting some money then?'

'Oh sure.' She didn't sound that convinced.

If he didn't get money, was he going to end up living here for ever? Now I had no problem with that, why should I? But it would be disappointing, all that talk of the brave new life. And Ian wouldn't be happy, not one little bit. And all those in the village who'd helped bring him in from the storm, or who'd given him credit—how pleased would they be, now the novelty had worn off?

But, despite my worries, things stayed calm. Ian put us down for the curragh race; and I let him. I reckoned I wouldn't disgrace us. Another half week went by and the night of the dance grew nearer. I spent my time practising for the gig, and saw little of Ian and nothing of Malouf or Anna or John. If I had, perhaps I might have been ready for the storm when it broke.

Eleven

I still couldn't catch the tune fully. It was right there but at the edge of me, you know, like when you have dots in your eyes from the sun and they keep slipping off to the edge of your vision.

The best place for practising, if it's too cold or windy to be up at the tower on the hill, is the little haybarn that we have at the back of the house. The weather had changed and from where I was sitting, in the back dark corner, I could still see out of the door and the sky was dull grey, heavy with rain it looked to me. For the time being the soft days had gone and that is the way it always is here, nothing is constant, except maybe people.

I gave up on my tune and went back to the songs I had to learn, running through them yet again. I was nervous about how I would perform on the night. Odd thing was that I'd not been at all worried when I first got the offer to play. Now I half wished that the gig wasn't in Aghleam but further up the Mullet where I wouldn't be so well known. The trouble was I'd begun to think that if this went well I could maybe cut a life for myself playing the fiddle. That would be something.

A shadow at the doorway made me look up. It was my dad, leaning against the doorjamb. I thought he'd come to listen but when I called out to him he sort of shook himself like a wet dog and drifted off. I didn't think he was well; he seemed to have no purpose in him. The busier my mother was with all her visitors and her precious John James making his stately visits out from Belmullet, the quieter himself was, taking his seat in the corner of the kitchen listening to the talk of women, losing colour in his face. I noticed it without taking it in, too busy with my own affairs. Isn't that always the story.

I put down the fiddle and went over to the door and watched him slowly walking up the lane. A drizzle had begun to fall softly, blurring the edge of things. The sky was hazy grey. The summer was slipping away and nothing was finished. Then as I stood there watching he slowed down and then, like a boat settling its keel down on to the mud, he began to heel over. Suddenly he went, flat, sideways and I lost sight of him.

I sprinted after him, leaping the gate, and pelting up the lane. 'Dad!' I yelled, half aware of Brede coming out of her doorway and Mary's voice behind me. He was lying very still, one arm thrown out sideways and the other caught under his hip. The side of his face was already shiny with the wet of the rain, and his startling blue eye was wide open but not focused on anything.

I knelt down beside him and touched his neck. It was warm and when I pressed under his chin as I had been taught I could feel his pulse beating. His eye blinked once, twice and he cursed softly to himself. I wasn't sure whether to move him or not, but when he cursed again, more forcefully, and tried to push himself up, I helped him roll over, and then sit.

'What happened to you?' I asked.

'Old age,' he said sourly, and Brede who was kneeling the other side of him now, laughed.

'You're the one,' she said.

'The one for Belmullet Hospital, you mean, God help me.'

'He's not going to be helping the likes of you.'

'Shut your gab, woman, and help me up.'

Not for the first time I felt out of place between the two of them. He and Brede shared something which went back way beyond me, and as my mother came bustling up, giving out instructions, way beyond her too. Dad and Brede were from the island, maybe that was all there was to it.

We half walked him, half carried him back into our house and laid him on his bed. After his first words to Brede he didn't open his mouth again, not that evening. He was building up strength, I suppose to put up with Mam's fussing.

I was sent off to phone the doctor but the doctor wouldn't come out to us. It was a better thing, he said, to bring him into the hospital, which I didn't argue with. Gary was rounded up, not from the pub but from the quay. He had taken to going out in one of the fishing boats.

After a load of fussing from everyone, Dad was shifted from his bed, and into Eamon's car. I wasn't allowed to go with them; there wasn't room. I watched the car bump up the lane, Dad's white head visible through the back window. Gary promised me he would take me in to see him the next day.

I felt as slate grey as the sky. I turned my collar up against the thickening drizzle and went looking for Ian but Brede said he was down in the village. She told me not to worry and made me sit and talk to her for a while but there was no comfort in talking to her because she didn't believe what she herself was saying.

'Your father is the strongest man I ever knew . . . No island man ever died from falling down in a muddy lane I can tell you that . . . ' She bustled and boiled the kettle and all she did was make me die to leave, which I did, blustering some excuse about having to get into Aghleam to phone.

I walked all the way and wasn't at all sure what I would do when I got there, except I thought maybe Ian would be at Barratt's helping out. I saw a car with an English registration drive through, heading out towards Falmore, the windscreen wiper clicking slowly to and fro and the people inside no doubt wishing they were somewhere else.

I was about to turn into Barratt's when I saw Malouf coming towards me. I hardly recognized him. His face was gaunt, and shiny with sweat. His eyes stared ahead of him like a simple man's. He was walking fast and God knows where he was heading, not in the direction of Anna's, that was for sure. I called him and waved, and though he looked my way he didn't appear to see me at all, and just hurried on. Thinking it more than strange I turned into the bar, hoping that Ian was there and that maybe he could tell me what was the matter.

As it turned out, Ian wasn't there, but I fell to talking with Mick who told me that the African was getting himself into people's bad books. 'Not paying his way,' he muttered. 'That's what most people say.'

Poor Malouf, no money had come through and all he had here was a wrecked boat. 'But surely the Macbraids were looking after him?' I said.

Mick pulled a face and gave the pint glass he was drying an overly careful wipe of the rim. 'I think his credit's about all used up.' It depressed me to hear him saying this and I turned to go. 'Sorry about your father, Willie,' he called out after me.

I let the door close behind me, and began to walk along the street. If even solid, reliable, fair Mick Barratt was turning agin our foreigner, maybe we weren't such a hospitable place out here on the western edge as we'd always prided ourselves on being. My thoughts were broken by the shrill ting of a bike bell and Ian squealing up beside me. 'I'd had half a mind to look for you,' I said.

His face was flushed from the cycling, his eyes pale. 'I thought you were set on becoming a monk,' said he.

'And why was that?'

'Lost to the world, is why. What have you been at?'

'Practising.'

'Is that so?'

It didn't take a bishop to tell he was in a bad mood but he dismounted and we walked together up the road to Glosh. He and Malouf had fallen out. Ian was all outrage. He had spent two full weeks guarding the yacht and not a penny to show for it. 'Sure the man is a fraud,' he said. 'I'll not believe a word he says again, not in a hurry.'

'And what of getting to Germany with him?'

Ian shrugged and pulled up his collar against the damp. 'He's no longer being put up by the Macbraids, you know. Anna won't have anything to do with him.'

Flighty Anna. 'That's hard, isn't it? He didn't ask to be wrecked on this bit of coast.'

'Life's hard,' said Ian flatly. 'And, anyway, that man tells lies.'

'What lies?'

'Ach, come on, Willie. All that guff he told us about the German tourist that became like a father to him, gave him the boat and all, I don't believe a word of it any more. I truly don't.'

'Maybe you're right,' I said, though I couldn't accept it, not wholly. Perhaps he was no prince from across the sea but nor was he a common cheat or crook, surely not. Ian thought different. His face was set hard and there was no arguing with him when he was like that.

We parted civil enough, agreeing to meet up first thing in the morning to try the circuit in the curragh and then leave the afternoon for me to go in to see Dad.

I slept badly, rose early, moved the cattle, then decided to cycle down to Blacksod ahead of Ian, maybe walk off whatever it was that was nagging at me. I met him at eight-thirty down at the shore. There wasn't any chat. Eight-thirty is early for both of us. Together we heaved the curragh down the slip and into the water.

I managed well enough until the wind began to get up. It

was sheltered where we were rowing, and the shore was close by but I could see waves breaking against the pier at Blacksod, and there were white horses, tipping their tails at me, beckoning to me, inviting me out into the deep water, and I began to get agitated.

'We're all right,' Ian snapped. 'One more time and try to get the rhythm this time, for Christ's sake.' A minute later: 'Willie, you're pulling like a cow.'

'That's as maybe, but I want to go in.'

I shouldn't have fretted; it was an on-shore wind, and we weren't going anywhere, but I was sick in my chest and felt like hitting him in the face he was being that stubborn.

We parted from each other with not very good grace. He hadn't once asked about my dad.

Gary had got the loan of an old banger and so he drove me into the hospital in Belmullet and the two of us went into the ward where Dad was stuck with a whole line of heavy-looking old men in striped jamas. He looked withered beside them. Gary joked with him for a while but it was not easy for Gary to be there, I could tell that, and he jumped at the chance to head off into town to do a few messages and take in a pint or two while waiting for me. I sat on the chair beside Dad's bed and we said very little for a while, but we had always had that trick, he and I, of not having to talk.

'Don't be like me,' he said after a while.

'How's that, Dad?'

He shook his head. 'There was a time when I could have done anything.' I could hear behind the words the rough suck of his breath. 'But I settled for less. Don't do that to yourself, Willie. You've talent, use it.'

'First time you've said that to me.' It was no accusation. Why should I be bitter? He'd always been the quiet one, keeping his head down. I'd never expected him to stand up to her when I was practising and Mam yelling for me to quit my din.

'I'm saying it now.'

He leaned his head back against his pillow and closed his eyes. 'I should have travelled. I should never have stayed in this place.'

'So you think John and Gary are right?'

'You could be different, Willie.'

I certainly could, the only one on the Mullet with a phobia about sea water and a knack for maybe offending the only good friend I was likely to have, though I still wasn't too sure where this shadow between Ian and myself had come from.

We sat quiet again and my father drifted into a shallow sleep. I stayed by his bed thinking about him and his life that was hidden from me. Maybe Mam knew why he was as he was and had never done more, maybe no one did. He stirred again when I got up to go. I pulled the blanket up over his thin chest and for a moment his speckled hand closed over mine. 'Hold on to the island land, Willie, never sell it, no matter what.'

'Do I have land out there, Dad? You've not said.'

'You do,' he said. 'You're the only one who does. John doesn't know that yet.' He barked a shallow laugh, halfway between a cough and a spit. 'And he won't like it either.' He closed his eyes. 'The islands never meant anything to him, nor Gary neither. You hold on to that bit of land we have.'

'I better go out there so.'

His eyes opened. Sharp blue. The hint of a smile. 'Do that.'

'All right.'

I walked out without looking back. I didn't want to see him among the other old men and them looking at me, like some odd fish.

I picked up Gary and we made our way home. I didn't mention what Dad had said.

There was a sharp west wind the next morning and the promise of worse to come, but our side of the Mullet was sheltered so Ian and I took the curragh out again. We rowed down as far as Elly Bay which was a major expedition as far as I was concerned, but we managed fine. We saw the yacht heeled over, but no sign of Malouf apart from a pair of shorts drying on a line.

We barely talked, the two of us, just concentrated on pulling together. The rhythm we struck was somehow cleansing; I felt tired but happier when we pulled into the slip. Ian smiled. 'I reckon we might do the race all right after all,' he said.

When I got home Mary had a message for me from the band, 'The Moonskinners' they were called. They were arriving at seven and they wanted me to be there prompt. Back came my nerves. I was down at Barratt's at five, sweeping the floor and for no money either.

The band were all college boys. Jimmy the bassist was my pal. I'd known him for years, the others were from beyond Crossmolina but they seemed friendly enough and were more than willing to let me have a go, having lost their own fiddler a month before. He'd gone to America for the summer vacation, good luck to him. We had a quick run through, acoustic, and then Mick gave them a meal.

It wasn't till nine that the pub began to fill, people streaming in, shaking the wet from their caps and coats, and it wasn't till ten that we started to play. There were a few shouts at me when I got up. To start with I was so nervous I could hardly count time. I kept my eye on the drummer and played safe until Jimmy mouthed at me to take a solo. I did and the floor was jumping, and I felt like I was flying on a high wind. After that, I began to relax. The music took me over, and, for the first time that night, I was able to look around.

There was Ian behind the bar, serving up pints, Anna dancing with Gary and that was a first for he never danced at all. John James and his Yankee friend were stuck at a table over by the door and though it was hard to see, I could swear that they were arguing, at least John was, his face looked black. But the crowd moved and I lost sight of them.

Anna swung by me and grinned and I nodded and stamped my foot, and my fingers found the notes without me thinking, or so it seemed. And then I saw Malouf. I didn't see him actually come in but there he was at the doorway dripping wet; the rain must have started to fall real heavily. He looked wild: his woolly hair had gone long and bushed out from his head like a black halo and his eyes were wide and round and crazy looking.

He was scanning the crowd. I knew he was looking for Anna. Then he suddenly forced his way through on to the dance floor and grabbed her by the shoulder, pulling her round. She winced and Gary pushed him away. But he didn't seem to notice Gary, which is a bit of a miracle, Gary being over six foot and built out of stone. Malouf had eyes only for Anna and he seemed to be pleading with her, trying to catch at her hand. Jeez but she looked cross, her eyes blazing. She swung at him and caught him a crack across the cheek and left him standing right under our little stage, looking lost and stupid while she shouldered herself away towards the door, Gary following.

A couple of lads gathered round Malouf and started to poke fun at him. One spilled beer on him, then pretended to apologize. Malouf hardly registered it at all. A dancer backed into him, and someone else jostled him and he seemed to be passed, hand to elbow, across the floor and over to the corner where I lost him for a moment.

The next thing I noticed was that there was no sign of Anna, and Gary, her knight in shining armour, was over at the bar refuelling himself. I saw the American standing up and putting on his jacket. John I couldn't see at all. It was weird.

I had half a mind to put my fiddle down and go out and look for her for I had a bad feeling, don't ask me why. But we were stuck into a rocking medley and there wasn't a break. I was caught in the pattern of sound, and held there, but the pleasure and excitement had gone; I was playing by numbers, aching for the break. I wanted to find Malouf before something really bad happened. I should have just quit, but then it's always easy to be wise after the event, so Brede says.

Twelve

What the hell! Bad weather clears the sky, that's what
Francis says.

The bass was threading my bones, the snare snapping the
back of my head, I closed my eyes and stamped my foot as
we tore into 'Johnny Boyle's Jig'.

'How's that, Willie!' someone shouted from the floor. I
opened my eyes and saw fat Mrs Dean in her white cardi
and black skirt, knee-stepping by in a mighty whirl, hands
clamped on to big Pat Flynn, our butcher and one-time
football hero.

'All right!' I yelled back, though already she was eaten up
in the crowd. A few of my mates from school had taken up a
stand at the edge of the stage and were bouncing up and
down as if we were a punk band. There was PJ, Jackie, little
Jean with the wire glasses, Mick Byrne, Ailish and Pat. The
biggest of them, Pat, already looked out of it.

I tell you the air was thick with drink and excitement, and
I almost thought I was king, stood up there beside Noddy
Wheelan the Moonskinner's guitarist. He grinned at me
and crashed out the last chord that brought the jig juddering
to a close. There was yelling and stamping of feet and shouts
of 'Get on with it, lads!'

I saw Ailish King and Jean Coyle grinning and waving at
me which took me by surprise a bit for Ailish usually gives
me a hard time at school. I kind of waved back all the same.

'Let's give it one,' said Jimmy.

We knocked out another jig and then slowed it down
because our drummer said he was knackered. We all were.
It was a soft, haunting air, one I didn't know. I moved to the

edge of the stage, letting my eyes stray over the crowd, picking out Ian at the bar, Brede in the corner, and John James, looking damp and dishevelled, his jacket slapped with mud. Where had he been? There was no sign of the Yank.

The bobbing and whirling had slowed to a loose swaying, then I saw the door open and there was Anna. I think I was the only one to notice her at first. She didn't crash in like some gunfighter in a western, just stood there, her shoulders hunched up, head down, hair plastered blackly to her face; her arms bare and her hands clasped tightly together and her shirt untucked and torn. My first thought was she had been knocked down by some drunken eejit, but then she looked up and I don't know what it was, but I knew something was badly wrong; something worse than an accident.

I'd a fear in my gut, like I get on the sea. I put down my fiddle and jumped from the stage.

'Ye're not packing it in,' Pat flung a drunken arm round my shoulder.

'Leave it, Pat. I'll be back in a minute.'

But the idiot wouldn't let go. His breath smelled of Harp, and his face had a stupid grin smeared across it. 'Up you go,' he kept repeating, pulling me back to the stage, the other lads jostling around me, all in good humour but on the edge, you know.

I've seen loud laughter turn to fists often enough, but I hadn't the patience to handle these bucks right. I swung myself free and, shoving Pat in the middle of the chest, sent him staggering back into the table behind him, and then cut through the dancers towards the door. I heard a shout behind me but ignored it.

'Mind the way now,' I said, pushing past the sweating dancers.

But I never got to her. There was a crash and an angry roar: 'By Christ, she's been hurt!'

'Who's that?'

'Anna Macbraid.'

There was a high wall of shoulders in front of me. 'Let me by.'

'Mind that, son.'

Then John James's angry roar again, for it was his voice I'd heard: 'Shut that band. Shut their damn noise!'

Voices were raised and the Moonskinners' song died with a last note on the bass and a reflex thump on the drum. And for the first time that evening there was a kind of silence of heavy breathing, and angry murmuring, with people not wanting to ask out loud what was going on but already warming up to trouble.

'For Christ sake, Willie, quit your shoving will you.'

I saw her, though there must have been a good fifteen or so people round her, clogging up the air with their concern. I saw her, her face white, one eye dark from where she'd been hit, blood on her shoulder showing through the white of her shirt. John had one supporting arm round her, and was edging her sideways towards the bar and maybe into the quiet of the snug behind. She wasn't looking at him, but at us, kind of wild but with no light in her eyes. It was terrible to see her like that.

'He did it to her!' shouted John. 'That—'

'Who?'

'That cursed African.' And then louder and with a kind of deliberate emphasis: 'That African attacked our Anna, that's what he did.'

The anger was thick now, and ugly as spit.

'He wouldn't have the nerve!'

'Call the gardai.'

'What do ye want the gardai for?'

I was caught in a surge towards the door and practically lifted off my feet. I hit the side of the door and then was shoved out into the dark and the sharp rain and I thought,

113

'Oh God, another black night just like when Malouf was driven in by the storm.'

And as I saw the men rolling out, faces moon white and mouthing curses, their voices flat and sweaty with beer, their breath heavy with the excitement of violence, I felt I no longer knew my own village, nor the people in it. There they were stumbling and ducking through the rain, banging on the roofs of cars, engines starting up, headlights poking into the rain-flecked dark. I stood there and tried to take stock. All I knew was that, innocent or guilty, Malouf was a dead man if any of the boyos found him.

Where would he be?

What had really happened?

Two more men came out, bottles of beer in their hands, laughing. 'Bit of sport, eh?' And then they stumbled off.

I turned in through the door. I hadn't seen Ian. Perhaps he'd caught more than me, seen what had led up to this. Perhaps Anna could tell us more? Mick Barratt was standing with his large bulk blocking the door to the inner room, a couple of ladies arguing with him, wanting to get by.

'She's within and she's all right, my missus is minding her. She don't need any more help. Go on home now, Caitleen.'

'Well, I hope you know what you are up to, Mick Barratt. Mrs Macbraid will not be happy if she hears you didn't let us in to see her only daughter, I can tell you that.'

'All right now, just go on home. I have the gardai called and the man responsible will be brought in. The doctor's on his way.'

Clucking furiously, the gaggle of women pushed by me. Mick sighed and wiped his thick forearm across his face. 'Are you there, Willie? I thought I saw you running out with all the other young bucks.' Over on the stage the band were packing up, tired, all the excitement drained into this terrible anticlimax.

'Is she all right?'

'She'll survive,' he said, his eyes avoiding mine. 'A few knocks is all.'

'Can't I see her, Mick? I want to know what happened.'

'We know what happened, Willie. That African friend of yours assaulted her. I saw the two of them arguing earlier in the evening myself . . . '

I had too. It was true . . . and yet, excitable as he was, I couldn't see him hurting anyone . . .

'The best you can do is go home, or find that madman yourself and get him back here before someone kills him.'

'Is that what she said, that Malouf attacked her?'

He poured himself a small glass of whiskey, and knocked it back in one gulp. 'It was your brother she told. Didn't you hear him, roaring like a bull?'

I'd heard him all right. I'd also seen him wet and scruffy from the rain and looking black and angry before Anna came in. 'His Yank friend, did you see him, Mick?'

'No, why?'

Perhaps things were as they seemed, the way everyone had taken them to be. I just didn't think so.

'Where's Ian?'

'I sent him to the Macbraid place so that her mother could come and fetch her back home after the doctor's seen her.'

'You have called the gardai?'

'Aye. God willing they'll be here before there's any more trouble.'

Jimmy and Noddy Wheelan struggled past with one of the amps. 'Give us a hand loading the van, Willie.'

'Sure.' Where would Malouf be hiding?

I took one end of the big amplifier and we wheeled it to the door, hefted it over the kerb and then into the van.

'You didn't tell me what Aghleam was really like, Willie.'

'It's not like this,' I said.

Noddy laughed. 'Is that right? Jeez do you remember the

Blues Brothers and that bar where they had to play behind a wire grille, you know—'

There was the sound of a bottle smashing and a shout and a couple of figures running unsteadily off round the back of the teacher's house.

'I wouldn't want that lot after me.'

'Me neither.'

We eased up the last of the equipment. I had to find Malouf and quick. 'I'll see you, lads,' I said.

'Yeah, be in touch, Willie, you played well. We'll do some gigs again,' said Noddy. 'Here,' he shoved fifteen quid into my hand. 'Your share. Good luck.' He swung up into the driver's seat. There was a wave of a hand through the window and the old van pulled out and headed into the night.

I'd no idea where to begin looking for Malouf; he could be anywhere, anywhere at all, that's what I was telling myself, out in that wet night, the orange lights of the van flickering out of sight. And you'll hardly believe this for it's comic. I was just standing there, staring after the van, and you know where the man was? Right at my feet stretched out flat on the wet road! He'd been hiding under the van!

'You must be crazy,' I said as he raised himself up. 'That van could have squashed you flat.' His eyes were white and frightened; he looked like some skinny cartoon, not real. I could almost imagine him having been run over, and then peeling up from the road like in a *Tom and Jerry*.

'They want to kill me,' he said hoarsely.

'Aye, they do. Let's go.' I took off my jean jacket. 'Here, put this over your head.'

There was a shout from across the road. 'Who are ye?'

'Willie Cormack and one of the band,' I shouted back.

'Hey, Willie, great gig,' and the group of black shapes reeled off.

I took Malouf's arm and pulled him after me, down

behind the pub. I reckoned most people being the worse for drink would stick to the roads and lanes and not be bothering themselves by fighting through hedges and fences, so that is exactly what we would do.

'We go back to the *Katya*,' he said.

'Maybe, but not yet. Through here, come on.' The ground was pure mud, squelching into my runners. I shoved open the gate to Barratt's field. There was a little bothy where he kept an old cart that I thought might shelter us, but I had to yank Malouf down into the lee of the hedge when I heard a crash and a couple of lads running towards us. Then the whoosh of flame and the little stone building glowing orange, and the bit of glass in its one window cracking. The lads whooped and giggled.

'Are you sure he was in there, Pat?' asked one of them.

'Cooked like a sausage now,' said one.

'Black puddin'!' said another, and then more laughter as they sloshed past us where we lay, our faces pressed down into the wet ground, no more than a couple of yards from them.

'Come on.' We had to get out beyond Aghleam, maybe find the gardai. At least they would keep him safe. That's what I thought.

We half ran, crouching all the time, through one field after another, till we were torn, and scraped, and muddied and the breath all sucked out of us so that we didn't so much speak as grunt. My sides were stapled with a stitch that ran from shoulder to hip and I was wet to the bone and colder than I can ever recall. He must have been worse. I was vaguely aware of the rasping sound of his breath and the chattering of his teeth and the hiss of the rain falling around us.

The night seemed as long as a hundred miles but at least we lost the sound of the searchers. I heard cars passing along the road once or twice, and I did see the lights of a garda car but we were travelling a couple of fields parallel to the road and too far off to run and flag it down. We rested up in a turf shed at the back of a house in the next village.

'William, the thief,' said Malouf after we had sat in silence catching our breath, easing our lungs and our bruises. 'You have saved my life I think.'

I think maybe I had, but the night wasn't over yet. 'Are you going to tell me what happened between you and Anna?' I said.

'Anna? Nothing. Nothing. She will have nothing to do with me,' he said.

'Did you attack her?'

'What you say!' Suddenly he was leaning forward to me, his face staring into mine and there was that knife gleaming in his hand. The Lord knows where that came from. He was full of surprises. I would say that if some laggards did catch up with him he would give an account of himself, drowned rat that he was.

'Steady now. Why else did you think they're all hunting you?'

The sudden flash of fire died out of him. 'I am tired,' he said.

That was no surprise.

'I could not hurt Anna. I wished to marry her. How can you hurt someone you love?'

I thought perhaps there were people who could do just that, but he wasn't one of them.

'Perhaps she will follow me to Germany,' he said after we had lapsed into silence, each of us lost in our own thoughts.

I didn't think this was likely and said as much. 'And I can't see you getting very far at all, not without a lot of help. When is your money coming in, Malouf?'

'No money. No wife. No boat . . . '

'I thought you were set up,' I said.

His white teeth gleamed in a smile. 'This is not the first

time I have to run, William. In my country there is a war, you know, and in my village anyone who does not support the Islamic fighters is *phshewed*.' And he tilted his chin and made a pretend swipe at his neck with the knife.

'And didn't you support them?'

'No. I didn't care about what they wanted. I wanted things for me. I was trapped there, only tourist visitors can come and go, tourists and the fighters, they had cars too.'

'And what about your German friend.'

'They kill tourists,' he said. 'A statement to our government. They kill tourists, policemen, anyone who collaborates with the government, they kill, and the government kills anyone who supports the rebels. That is the way it is.'

I frowned. 'What you told me and Ian before, Malouf, was that not true?'

'What is truth? You see me. I have a boat. I am sailing to Germany. That is true.'

'But is that boat yours?'

'You think I am a thief?'

'I don't know what I think.'

'They killed my German friend, my father. They shot him in the white Mercedes I was driving for him. They shot him while I was at the wheel, and I knew they were going to shoot him. I had told him so but he would not listen. He said we must go up into the mountain, and they had a camp there. I had been to it . . . '

'You had been one of the fighters, hadn't you?'

'They never let you go, and I tried to go. I am not a killer. I could not do the things they wanted, the bombs, the terror . . . you know they can follow a man even in London, New York, they will track down their enemies and kill them.'

'Not here they couldn't.'

'No, here others will do that for them. We must go back

and see Anna. She will know I did nothing to hurt her.' He stood up.

'Don't be crazy. You can let the gardai sort it out. Come morning there will be nothing of this left but a lot of people with hangovers. Surely she knows it wasn't you that attacked her—' I stopped. Of course she should know, so why hadn't she said anything? Why had she told John . . . Had she told John anything? Was John covering something up? I remembered the way he'd looked; the argument he seemed to be having with the Yank; and the sudden disappearance of the Yank.

I looked across at Mal; his arms were folded round his knees, his head bent forward, staring at nothing. 'I bet it was the Yank,' I said. He looked at me blankly. I recalled the way she had travelled in the car with them to Blacksod and the way the Yank had talked to her, and eyed her. Sure John was covering up for him, too important a contact for him to lose to the police. You don't get the best kind of investments if your investor is in prison for attempted rape.

I didn't even like to think it, but that was it, wasn't it? Rape. I could just hear John James laying it on thick to the gardai, and Malouf would be the right scapegoat. Oh yes. That made a kind of sense.

I kept quiet. What was the point in telling him; he'd go crazy and run smack into someone who'd use a bottle rather than a brain; and what was already bad would turn worse. We drifted off into an uneasy sleep, turf dust blotting up the dampness of our clothes, gritting its way into our hair and eyes. But at least we were out of the wet and the cold, and, for the time being, safe.

Thirteen

The voices came murmuring out of the darkness, threading in with the rain still drumming lightly on the roof of the shed, and I didn't know whether I was rightly sleeping or not. I was half aware of the lumpy turf digging into my hips, there might have been the scuffle of feet, and the bang of the door, or maybe it was the wind but, voices or no, I sank swiftly back into the black . . .

. . . Down and down into the black water.

I've tried describing the dream, but I can never make it sound how it really is, for it has no beginning and no end, and it's not always the same, and there is nothing distinct, only shapes that move, bend and change, like shadows except they're not shadows but people who flow in and out of the edge of darkness, like seaweed shifting with the tide. Sometimes, though, there's the white head of a breaking wave towering above me, and then in my ears there's the shrieking roar of water, and I wake gasping. I always wake gasping, and flailing to rise up, up . . . my chest burning from the lack of air.

Imagine yourself under water, the surface shifting and breaking just above you. You can almost reach it except there's something holding you, pulling you down. You can feel it gripped around your ankle, cold and hard; and though you want to be looking up, you turn your head down and peer into the thickness of the water, knowing that those shapeless figures will be swaying at you, and they are. But worst of all is what you see coming out of the darkness. It is a single hand. You can see every hair and blue-black blemish on that white hand. The fingers hard and knotted, the tendons on the wrist, swollen with the effort, the effort to pull you down into deep . . .

And that is how I woke on that morning after Malouf and I lit out of Aghleam in the storm. There was grey light filtering into the turf shed from under the door, and I was sucking air into myself and then spluttering till my eyes watered, for my face was stuck sideways into the turf dust and I half choked myself to death.

When I'd caught my breath, I wiped the dust from my mouth, and then, with the inside tag of my T-shirt, the water from my eyes. For a moment, I didn't know where I was at all—and then it was clear enough, clear enough I was on my own. Where the divil had he gone?

I opened the door, quiet like, and took a peek outside. It was early and there was no sign of life in the house, so I slipped out. Not a sight of him anywhere, only the wet grass, and a few cattle, their breath steaming, looking idly my way.

It was then I remembered the voices in the night. But maybe it had just been Malouf himself telling me something? Sure it was more like to have been that, who else would go rattling around in a turf shed in the middle of the night? He must have headed out to the boat. He'd be safe enough out there, and comfortable too; and I cursed him for not waking me.

I had nothing but the clothes I'd slept in, the T-shirt and my jean jacket, damp from the night's rain. I turned up the collar on my jacket and slipped round the side of the house and then down on to the road. One way led to Elly and then on to Belmullet and the other back to Aghleam, and since that was the shorter way, for we had only gone about three miles in the night, though it had seemed closer to twenty, that was the way I began to walk.

I wasn't too worried about Malouf. I could hardly believe what I had seen last night and put it down to drink and mischief and that whoever the blackguard was that had set on

Anna, she'd be in a better state this morning to say who it was. It wouldn't be Malouf that she'd be naming—couldn't be.

And yet she'd struck him. I'd seen that. The two of them exchanging cross words, and then Anna cracking him across the cheek, and he not even flinching, just looking at her dead straight on. But that was the extent of it. Surely? But then why hadn't she stopped the mob baying after him?

Because she hadn't been there to stop them, had she? She had been taken into the back room, with John James throwing his weight around as usual. That was it. I determined that the first thing I had to do was to call up to Anna and see whether she was all right and find out who had set on her. God, it was an ugly business.

It's a lonely time out here at six o'clock of a morning, when the sky is flat and grey, and the sea stretches across the bay, the same slate colour as the sky, and the wind has all died away. In the distance I heard a lone dog barking, and one house to my right had a thin trickle of smoke from its chimney to show that at least one soul on the peninsula was stirring; everything else was still.

I liked Malouf and I hated what I'd seen in the village—but it only showed me how little you could know anyone. I didn't trust John or his friend; but sure I could be wrong. I liked Mal but how well did I know him?

The walking warmed me up a little and after an hour I reached the village and picked up my bike from the back of Barratt's where I had left it the night before. It was too early to call on Anna, too early to face a row with my mother who would be ready to crucify me for being out all night.

But there was nowhere else to go but home and so that's where I headed, thinking that I could slip in and get some dry clothes on before she stirred. I would tell her I'd gone off with the band, just for the crack. It wouldn't stop her shouting at me but it would be better than telling her that I'd been mixed up in that riot.

The back door was locked and my window was shut; Gary was too much of a slob to notice the need for fresh air, but the kitchen window was open and I got in easy enough, took out some dry clothes, let myself out and changed in the hayshed. Seven o'clock. I reckoned that Brede might be stirring, if not I'd rouse Ian and at least get myself a cup of tea there. So I went over to their house, and sure enough Brede was there, raking out the fire, her head lumpy with rollers under a blue scarf, and a red quilt dressing gown on her that might have suited a cardinal.

'Did the devil get you?' said she.

'No, but he half starved me.'

'You look sick.'

I'm sure that I did for my head was pounding and my mouth dry. She took me in and sat me down and asked me nothing until I had some tea inside me.

'Poor girl,' she said, sitting herself down at the table opposite me. 'That'll put an end to her fine airs and graces, I'd say.'

She could be sharp, Brede, but that was her way, and she always said what no one else would dare. 'What do you mean?'

She shook her head. 'Did it really happen, Willie? Did someone really set on her?'

'I told you! Her shirt was half torn from her back and she was wild upset. How could someone make up something like that?'

'But was it bad?' she said. 'You know.'

I knew.

Rape.

I was no baby. It happened. It happened in the quiet of little country towns not just in the bad cities. There was maybe nothing uglier and more frightening. Had it happened to Anna? How could I know; she was upset and crying all right but I didn't know. I didn't.

I shrugged and stirred my tea to avoid looking at her. 'Nobody waited to find out. Just ran out roaring. I don't know, Brede. She was shook, anyone could tell that, and frightened . . . ' I ran my thumb nail down a groove in her kitchen table. Most things in our house are plastic or shiny. Brede likes wood, even bits that are no good for anything, bits found on the beach or bleached oak roots dug out of the fields. 'All I know is that Malouf didn't have anything to do with it.'

'Why're you so ready to leap to his defence?'

'For the same reason half the village wanted to hang him with no right reason.'

She thought for a while on this, pouring herself a cup and looking out of the window towards the islands which were just duskily emerging from a thin sea mist. 'You're not that sick,' she said eventually.

I think she was about the most independent person I knew. She had no time for gossip or for fitting in with what everyone else might feel. That's why she and my mother weren't as close as such close neighbours ought to be, and maybe there were other reasons too why they didn't sit in each other's kitchens, like Mrs Macbraid and Mrs Barratt did.

I stood up to go.

'What will you do?' she asked.

I told her that I wanted to see Anna and try to find the truth of what happened.

'Didn't the sergeant call on her yet?'

'Mick Barratt said he called them out. But I don't know what happened.'

She sniffed.

'You don't like Anna much, do you?' I said.

'She's a tease. Wave a red rag long enough and a bull is going to charge.'

'That doesn't make it right.'

'Don't be stupid, boy. Nothing can make evil right, but that's no reason to shut your eyes to the way folk behave.'

I didn't argue with that. She thought it right too that I should go and see Anna, whether the sergeant had called or not. Sure I wanted to see her anyway but I also wanted her to clear Malouf in case any buck wanted to carry on the mischief of the night before and make the poor man's life a misery.

We talked about Dad then. She'd planned to go in to see him first thing so I said I'd go with her. Then Ian came in, tousled with sleep and sullen as a hog. He's never great first thing, so I left them, not saying to Ian where I was going, but promising to be back in an hour or so. I took the bike and cycled up the lane, round the hill, and then down into the village.

It is quite a steep path up to the Macbraid house, so I dumped my bike by the edge of the road and then found myself hesitating. What do you say? Are you all right? How're you, Anna? Mrs Macbraid, can I speak to Anna . . . I had myself in such a twist of words that by the time I was up at the door, and Anna standing there in front of me, a man's check shirt buttoned to the neck and her rich black hair scraped back into a ponytail, I couldn't say a stim.

'Willie!' She smiled.

'Are you OK?'

'Fine.'

When she turned her head sideways slightly to call back to her mother who it was, I could see a dark bruise down on the side of her face by her ear, and the knuckle on her right hand holding the door looked red and grazed. She noticed me looking.

'I didn't know I could punch but I caught him a real crack. I thought I broke me own hand.' She slowly clenched her fist and studied the knuckles. She hardly seemed that put out about what had happened.

'Who was it, Anna?'

She looked over my shoulder. 'I can't be sure,' and I just knew she was avoiding telling me.

Mickey, her little brother, came and hung on her legs, staring up at me, and then stuck out his tongue.

'Have you talked to the sergeant?' I asked.

'Why should I want to do that?'

'Didn't the gardai come out?'

She shrugged. 'Aye, but I wouldn't see them. There were no charges, Willie.'

'But you can't have people doing what happened last night.'

'I don't want to talk about it.'

'Don't you know what happened . . . you know, afterwards.'

'I said I don't want to talk about it.' There was an edge to her voice that I had never heard in her before.

'They were all after Malouf. They would have battered him if they'd caught him.'

'Did they catch him?' She didn't sound as if she cared too much one way or the other.

'No. And it wasn't him, was it?'

She hesitated. 'It could have been. It was that dark . . . I don't want to talk about it.'

She was lying. She knew it wasn't him. I couldn't believe it. 'What's got into you, Anna? You have to say. If you don't think it was him you have to say. They'll never leave him alone unless you say.'

'That's his lookout. Maybe he's outstayed his welcome in the village and I think maybe you've outstayed yours, Willie.' She made to close the door.

'All right,' I said holding up my hands. 'I didn't want to argue with you. I really didn't.'

'Go away, Willie,' hissed Mickey from behind her leg. She tousled his hair.

' . . . I'm glad you managed to hit the fella.'

Her smile came back. 'Yes.'

'Did you wind him?'

'In the face, I reckon.'

'Well done yourself.' I stepped back. I had all I wanted to know. 'If there's anything I can do to help.'

'Sure, Willie.' She lifted her hand and then ushered the little scut back into the house and I turned and walked down the path to my bike.

Funny how small moments can change you. I felt different that morning after meeting Anna. Maybe it's the feeling you get when you stop loving someone. Ah well, I thought, there's someone in the village sporting a mark on their face. It should be easy enough to clear Malouf now.

I would see my father, then Malouf, then get Ian to help me track down the man who'd started it all. He'd be good for that, Ian. And then I'd have words with that brother of mine and all, for rousing everyone up. I'd make him apologize to Malouf. Apologize! He would eat dirt. I'd make him. He wouldn't like that, not at all. It put a smile on my face. How the mighty will be fallen.

It turned out that no one at home had any intention of going in to see Dad that day: the Stations of the Cross were to be held in our house and my mother had the girls working at the cleaning so that neither priest nor neighbour would find a spot out of place.

Gary might have come (he surely would not have been seen dead lifting a helping hand in the house) but all I could get out of the darkened bedroom was a groan, and I had no intention of wasting half the day waiting on him to work off his hangover, so I left them all at it and called up to Brede.

She was out of the dressing gown, and into what she called her town gear: black shoes, black skirt, black cardigan. You'd think she was going to a funeral and not visiting a sick friend. Still, that was Brede. She went back in for her bag and I went to look for Ian.

He was round the back, tinkering with his bike.

'The gig was good,' he said without looking up, the way he did when concentrating with his hands.

'Are you telling me I was brilliant?'

'I never said that.'

I paused, watching him the while. 'It was a bad do, wasn't it?'

He knew what I was talking about. 'Aye.'

'I didn't see you when it all went mad.'

'I got out of there and came home. Ye can ask Auntie, if ye like . . .'

'I'm not interrogating you.'

I heard Brede calling me. 'Ah well, I'd best be off,' I said. 'I'll catch up with you later.'

'What about you,' he said. 'What did you do? Did you help in the hunt?'

'Are you kidding or what? I helped him get away. They'd have slaughtered him otherwise.'

'Did you?' He looked round at me then. 'Good on you, Willie. But I'd keep that under your hat.'

There was an odd note to his voice that made me stop. 'What are you on about?'

'Nothing. Only I wouldn't breeze it around, you know.'

Brede and I were lucky in picking up a lift straight off. We met Francis at the post office at ten o'clock and since he was driving into Belmullet on business he was happy to take us with him.

I sat quiet in the car while they chatted and I looked out at the soft way the land falls down to the sea, the green lanes winding away from the road, like veins on a giant's arm; a great arm hooked out into the sea, scooping the bay into us.

I looked and I thought about Ian. I was glad he'd had no part in the mischief.

Brede wanted to see my father first, and on her own, so I wandered round town for a bit, checking out the videos in the three shops that rent them, the same number as there are butcher's shops, and wishing that we had one of them video machines. It's not true you don't miss what you have never had. Still, maybe it wouldn't be so great in our house; we argue enough about the programmes on television; it would be hopeless deciding on what film to rent.

I gave Brede her half hour and then I went up to the hospital and along to his ward. She wasn't there, and since I didn't pass her, she must not have stayed as long as she had intended. But Dad was looking good, propped up in his bed, clean shaven, his eyes bright, and though I could hear the wheezing it wasn't so bad as before. I reckon he was pleased to see me. I nodded to the man beside him, and pulled up the chair so we could talk easy.

He was feeling a whole lot better and though Dr Ryan was talking about a bypass operation, he wouldn't consider it. 'When the ticker goes, Willie, I'll stop and sure that is the way God intended.'

Well, there are quite a few things you can say to that, namely what about all them powerful medical discoveries, and triumphs of the last forty years or so, but this was hardly the time for debate. So we talked about other things, Malouf for one. I wanted to know what we could do for him. My fear was that if he stayed, he would never get the money to launch and refit his yacht and, more to the point, the longer he stayed the more trouble there was going to be.

'That man,' said my father, 'is on a journey. He's come this far, and I'd say he will get to where he wants to go, boat or no boat. Perhaps he could get some money by salvage. The boat must be worth a fair bit: the engine, the fittings, you know . . . ' But when I told him about what had happened the previous night, he was for Malouf leaving right away.

We talked about the family a bit, and then I found myself telling him about my dream. I'd never described it to anyone before, but I told Dad now, and he listened and never said a word, though he nodded once or twice like he was recognizing something in what I said, though I can't see how that could be at all.

'You have a terrible fear, Willie,' he said at length, 'terrible. But you are an island man in your bones and you will have to beat it. The way I have found things is that there's never anything so bad that you can't face it, and when you face it enough times, the fear goes away bit by bit. Never completely maybe but enough to manage it. Like dying, you know—'

'You're not dying!'

He smiled. 'Maybe not.' He was tiring though. He let his head back against the pillow and closed his eyes for a moment. 'Go out to south island,' he said after a moment, 'and raise the godstone. That'll cure you of your dream, and, my God, it will help your friend on his journey. There was never real bad luck came to the island until that priest, Father O'Reilly, curse him, had the godstone thrown into the channel between the two islands. If you could find it, it would be a great thing.'

I wasn't sure that he was entirely talking sense about the stone, and I was having to lean towards him to hear what he was saying so I took his hand. 'I'll go now.'

'No.' He tightened his fingers round my hand. 'I'll tell you this. I'll tell you what I told no one else. Wait now and listen.'

131

Fourteen

And this was the story that my father told me. He spoke slowly, and with some difficulty, having to pause and catch his breath from time to time.

Our house, he said, was the very first one you would get to coming from the pier of Porteenbeg where we had our little harbour. You've not seen it yet so I'll tell you and ye can recognize it when you land and know that that's where your family came from for many long years. The pier itself is fine and wide and gives great shelter and all you need to do is walk the length of it, across a strip of sandy turf and there our house is. No longer white but grey, all the lime washed away by the weather; at one time all the houses round the bay were shining white.

There were six of us children and my mother and father, both dead, as you know, God rest their souls, living in that house. We had but the two rooms, and we kept them neat, I'm telling you. From our front door you could look across to Rusheen where the whaling factory was but that had long closed even when I was a small boy.

The year I'll tell you about was 1927.

I was ten and my father had started taking me out in the curragh, though my mother had complained that I was too young for fishing. But I was raring to join him for I reckoned him to be the best of all the fishermen on Inishkea South. You wouldn't mind any of the boats from the north island, they were never a match to ours.

He was a gentle man, my father, not big but fierce strong,

hands that when he lifted you up to swing you high, were as steady and strong as the hoops of iron you would find holding a keg of beer; though he always held us just so, never tight enough to show a mark. My father never raised a hand to any of us, though I know he was in a fair few scuffles with men from the north island when they had drink taken.

My mother wasn't an island woman at all, but came from Aghleam itself. He met her at a dance and carried away her heart. That's what she told us when we were little and we always wondered what she meant by it, for it sounded a thieving sort of thing to do. Mostly island men married island women and so my mother was different, red hair the colour of sunsets and a strong singing voice and great humour. She could laugh with and at anything and often did. She loved the island but she feared the sea. You and she would have had much in common, Willie, and you would have loved her as I did. It killed her to leave the island, but her heart was broken before that, and her spirit too, God love her.

And this is the day that killed her.

It was June and breathless hot. The sea was so hard flat and blue you'd almost think you could drive across it in a pony and trap, and the beach of Porteenbeg gleamed it was that hot and that white.

My father and I were working at the net, checking it and fixing it where it was torn. I had my back to the curragh, and a straw hat on that my mother made me wear, and my brothers were laughing at me from the doorway for wearing the hat. But I never heeded them for I knew they were jealous that I had man's work to do and they had none.

I don't remember who gave the call, but I do remember seeing the birds out over the water, maybe a mile off shore, wheeling and diving in a real fret of agitation—I'd never seen them like that before. And the call was that the salmon were running.

I don't think my father had wanted to go out that day. He said he didn't trust the heat, though I don't know why. But with the prospect of fine salmon fishing there would be no waiting. There were twelve curraghs at that time and within five minutes every one of them had two men, or a man and boy, straining at the oars and pulling out into that flat sea, my father and myself along with them, out towards where the birds were.

Now every year the salmon ran, down along the coast between the islands and the Mullet, looking for the estuary to the Owenmore and the Owenduff rivers. We had no big long nets to set like they do now and we could only draw quite shallow, so it would depend on how the fish were running as to how well we did.

That day was a miracle, we thought, for they were right up on the surface. The sea was broken with their silver leaping and splashing and we were like a pack of black wolves or hunting dogs closing in on the wide, moving shoal. And as soon as the first boat was there, out was flung the net and no sooner was it in the water than it was hauled back, streaming with fish.

'Take the oars, Mikeen!' my father said, 'while I handle the net.' He had it all neat and coiled down beneath the thwart and he picked it up and flung it in a wide, opening arc, while I pulled steady enough but without any great speed in the direction we wanted. And just like we had seen with the other boats, within seconds the net was full and dragging at the boat so that I could hardly pull against the weight at all, and the muscles on my father's arms were tight and straining as we heaved in the net.

You could hear shouting and laughing across the water from all the boats, and calling to each other, exclaiming at the miracle that was in the day to get such a catch as this. Out spilled the fish, flopping and slapping around our bare feet, and my father with his wooden peg, catching them

134

and belting them on the head and then flinging them up into the bows; and though some were no more than five or six pounds weight, there were a couple that were near twenty. 'We'll be taking these to the mainland, Mikeen,' said my father, 'and we'll make a few bob.'

Out went the net again and again, he hauled in a great scoop of fish. Now this was beginning to weigh us down, and indeed the boat nearest us was so heavy with fish that she was taking in water and Paddy Barratt and his brother were hard at work bailing to keep themselves afloat. I could hear them arguing as to whether they should go for one last haul.

I pulled us out a wee bit further from the other boats, the sweat pricking my back, and then I rested and was thankful, I can tell you, that my mother had given me the broad straw hat. My father was leaning over the stern. I can remember the very way his arms looked, shirt sleeve rolled, elbows bent out, forearms brown, knuckles white around the transom. I remember thinking, why was he holding on so tight and I realized that instead of looking down my father's head was tilted up, up at the sky to the south of the island. And then he gave a great shout: 'Storm! Cut your nets! Storm!'

There was nothing ever like it. Nothing. The sky was a wall of black, rolling towards us so fast that even as my father was out with his knife and hacking at the line to loose the net, the tip of the island was gone. And then just ahead of the darkness came the wind, cooler, hissing across the sea like the breath of a witch, whipping up short little waves, creaming them into horses; and then the waves ridged up all of an instant, getting steep.

I heard shouts and just before the light failed, I caught sight of poor Paddy and his brother. Instead of cutting the net free they had tried to haul in their final catch. They were down so low that when the first big wave rolled in on them, the curragh just went up on her tail. For the spit of a second, I saw Paddy up to his waist, and the tip of the curragh above him, and his poor brother who'd been up in the bows as a counterweight thrown clear over the side. And then they were lost and there was no more sight of them, nor of the others.

It was black night then and sometimes I think that is how hell must be, roaring black with white angry bursts of waves twenty foot above your head, threatening to crush you every moment.

My father moved swiftly. 'In the stern, Mikeen, right down now,' he said, his voice raised loud against the sound of the wind. 'Throw out the fish and bail water as hard as you can.'

I did what he told me, all them beautiful salmon, some still with life in them, one after the other, until my right hand was slippery with fish slime. And he was at the oars, rowing hard, bending into the task like that Hercules fella. Our curragh lifted and spun like a wild horse. One minute we'd be almost straight up and then we'd be atop the wave and coursing down, my father pulling hard, first with one oar, then the other, steadying, straightening, and then both together, short and hard, his face grim, concentrating; and all the time bearing towards the harbour.

We weren't that far you see, not really, and when I caught the glimmer of lights from Porteenbeg, pricking through the black spray, I sang out to my father that we were near home. Another hundred yards maybe and we would have had enough shelter from the wind to make it into the harbour, another hundred yards is all.

I saw the pier and, by God, I saw the women and the sight of them frightened me for they were like lost souls, Willie, their shawls and skirts whipping around them, as they gathered at the very point of the pier, and their faces white and them shouting and wailing and we not able to hear a word from them.

So close we were, but cursed too, for the wind had the very divil in it. Just like that, it switched right round to the west so that we were head on to it and my father hadn't the strength to fight against it.

'Cursed luck, Mikeen,' he said and spun the curragh round on the top of a wave so that we streamed down with it. 'We can only run ahead of the storm now. Keep bailing for if we stay afloat with God's love we'll end on the mainland.'

I didn't cry, though I think I knew we had little hope, either of us, of making it to safety. But without question I worked hard at the bailing, using the leather bucket my father had fashioned and always kept lashed to the boat— there were not that many as careful as my father. Most of the men were casual, you know, and thought nothing of using their hands to bail, or a cap. Poor souls, they were the first to drown in that storm.

I remember the cold then, after that terrible heat, and I remember my father hardly rowing, using the oars only to steady us and straighten us, and pulling hard only when a breaking wave threatened to swamp us. And we were swamped time after time, but I bailed us clear enough to keep afloat.

That night seemed to last forever and though I thought the wind was all the time blowing from the same quarter, I was that exhausted I couldn't be sure. My fear was telling me that maybe it had swung round, like one of them hurricanes and was lashing us out into the mighty Atlantic itself.

I was more tired than I had ever been, my eyes stinging from the salt and the strain of all the time peering ahead into the dark, hoping for land and yet fearing that I'd hear the louder roar of waves on rocks. For though it was a thin chance that we would stay afloat till we reached the mainland it was thinner still that we would be flung up on the strand at Caricklahan . . . and between those bays were the Mullet's teeth that would grind us to pulp and spit us back into the ocean. But my father said nothing of this, and nor did I, for always there is hope.

One of the last things he said to me that night was, 'We can't be far now, Mikeen. You're doing great.'

Then, by Christ, a fearful thing happened: a black shape, blacker than the waves or the night, loomed way over us, and I thought it was Jonah's whale come to swallow us up. 'Father!' I yelled and pointed and he turned his head, and gave a mighty sweep of his left oar that spun us out of the way of the careening curragh bearing down on us. It swept past, rolling over, monstrous and broken and yet if it had hit us it would have been our death, right then. But the danger was not over, not at all. Listen to this.

We saw a face in the water, upright in a wave, rising above us. I thought it was the sea fairies come to take us down. Perhaps it was, though, if so, they had taken the shape and face of Michael John Maguire, one of the young men out fishing with us and a cousin to my father, and a dear friend of his. It was his boat that had been flung aside by the storm, and he and his partner (though we saw no sign of him) must have been following the same path as ourselves, hoping to beach on the mainland. I swear to God I saw Michael's mouth move, trying to tell us something, though himself was under water, and his face bursting.

'Jesus Christ!' shouted my father, and he never swore once in his entire life. 'Jesus Christ, Mikeen, 'tis poor Michael.' And Michael's hand was stuck right out of that wave and my father without a moment's thought leaned right out to it and gripped it into his own. The curragh gave a lurch and I watched in horror as my father was pulled right out over the side, and the two of them there, hand in hand, sank into the deep . . .

'Two good men, Willie, and my father was a beautiful man and that is the truth, and the sea swallowed him right up.' Dad sighed and looked at his own hands, and I, sitting there beside him in the hospital, took one of them into my own, and it was warm and dry and he didn't smile but closed his blue eyes and I thought he was going to sleep, but a moment later he continued with his story.

I cried then, for fear and loneliness, and I let the sea do what it liked for I could never manage those oars, not in that weather. And I was spun this way and that and I just kept a tight hold to the sides of the curragh and shut my eyes and prayed and prayed. And God surely heard my prayers for I remember suddenly picking out the sound of water beating against the shore, and then a great wave took the boat. By some stroke of luck the curragh was well balanced and came tearing down that wave, but I knew this was the last one for me, and sure enough the curragh slewed to the side and I was pitched right out into the water. I almost felt relief that it was over.

Can you imagine my surprise then when, hard under my hands and knees, I felt sand. Another wave broke and rolled me under and along, and I lay exhausted and might have drowned there but something urged me to crawl a little further and I did, and there I think I passed out. The next thing I remembered was a grey dawn rising and stiffness in my bones and me creeping up from the beach to a cottage and knocking on the door and the woman of the house exclaiming when she saw me. She brought me to the warmth, and rested me then by the fire with a blanket round my shoulders and a cup of tea in my hand and I told her and her husband there my story. And they both shook their heads and blessed the poor drowned souls for they knew that I was only telling the truth.

And so my father's story ended. And I knew why he had told me it, for, strange as it sounds, it had something of my

139

dream in it: the waves curling, the dark water and the drowning men. And yet that terrible night didn't seem to haunt my father. Where did my fear come from?

'Listen to me, Willie,' he said. 'That tragedy broke the heart of the island. So many young men drowned, but I survived and so did two brothers who were brought up on the same strand as myself. And if there had been more who had loosed their nets when my father first called, who knows, maybe more would have stayed afloat and so had a greater chance of reaching the shore. But remember this, Willie,' he said, looking at me full, his eyes the colour of summer sky, 'if there are drowned men in your dream, they are all your friends, all your family. And my father is there with them, God love them all, and live or die they will only care for you.'

He released my hand. 'Lift up that godstone and maybe it will bring some life back into the islands. That would be a great thing.'

His eyes closed then and I left him, and the hospital, and found Brede and Francis waiting for me in the car down at the gate and we drove the long road home.

Not one of us talked until we reached Elly Bay and I asked Francis to let me off there. I thanked him and he said, 'Good luck, Willie,' but he didn't mean anything weighty by that. It was just his way.

Fifteen

The *Katya* had shifted slightly in the storm of the night before and was now in closer to a spine of rocky land at the end of the bay. She'd twisted round too, so that her tall mast pointed helplessly in towards the land: even from where I was standing on the strand you could see that she was a yacht going nowhere. She'd never get to sea again. I don't know why I was so sure, just the feeling you get when something is broken inside.

I gave a shout and then another but there was no answering call, nor any sign of a black head peering out of the cockpit. Sure Malouf had to be there, where else would he have gone? I called a third time.

A tractor rumbled down the road behind me, while I was wondering what I should do or whether I should wade out; and then a man on a bicycle came by and then stopped.

'That's a sorry sight,' he said.

'It is.'

I wanted to give another shout but I felt foolish standing on the strand with this man watching, myself yelling to a silent wreck.

'I heard that this black man was carrying a whole load of drugs,' he said, 'all the way from Africa.' He came from Saleen, I recognized him well enough though I didn't know his name.

'Is that right?'

'That's what I heard.' He nodded and rubbed a hand over the frosty white stubble of his chin. 'Though why any man would be bringing drugs here I cannot think. Still, they say 'tis a terrible problem in Dublin and Cork and maybe in Ballina too, all them cities.'

I agreed that maybe it was a problem but that as far as I or anyone else knew the African had only been bringing himself. This didn't convince the old man.

'Do you take them drugs yourself?' he said.

'Go on,' I said. 'I do not.' And because I was near certain that he would be happy to carry on talking for another half an hour or so, I did what I now knew I was going to have to do anyway and kicked off my shoes and laced them round my neck. I didn't bother to roll up my jeans, I was going to get wet and that was it.

'Are ye going in for a swim?'

'I am.'

I stepped out and felt the water on my feet, soaking my jeans. I kept my eyes fixed on *Katya* and waded slowly. I didn't want to slip. If I lost my footing I would surely panic. The thought of water covering my face actually made me stop, freeze, you know. Funny thing was it was the old fella on the shore that kind of aggravated me into keeping going.

'Are ye soft in the head, laddy, swimming in the clothes that you're wearing?'

I gritted my teeth and didn't make the rude retort that was on my lips and a moment later I heard the rattle of his bike and I pushed on. It's not so terrible, I kept telling myself. In truth, it wasn't either and though I got myself wet to the waist, just as I had the first time Ian and I had come to the boat, I suffered nothing worse than that.

The boat was no more than twenty yards or so from the shore at this stage of the tide and when I finally reached her side, I gripped the rail and hauled myself up. 'Hey, Malouf,' I called out. No response. Maybe he thought I was one of a gang from the night before, hunting him down, so I called again to reassure him, though I sort of knew in my bones that there was no one aboard. 'It's me, Willie,' I said, but there was still no response.

The sails were all wrapped, and ropes stowed but there was still a kind of shabby, beaten look about the slanting deck: the brass was salty green, the varnish on the woodwork white and flaky, and the cockpit had a pool of water in the tilt of it. I knocked on the little door to the companionway—not that I expected to hear his voice now—and then pulled it open.

All was shipshape below. Ian had kept below decks well in his nights out here. I sat down on the bench seat and tried to figure out where that strange man would have gone to. Why get up in the middle of the night from where we had been sheltering? Why not tell me? Jesus, hadn't I been the one to help him? What was he at?

I got up, one hand on the companionway to steady myself. You'd go crazy living at an angle like this all the time, sort of like being in a crooked dream. Maybe that was why Ian was quiet in himself. Perhaps Malouf had decided to go to Belmullet, or see Francis, or even report the incident of the night before to the gardai, so I went back up on deck only to be greeted by jeers and catcalls from a gang of lads on the beach.

'You'll not find the black out there, Will Cormack!'

What did they mean by that? 'He'll be back soon enough,' I said.

One of them said something I couldn't hear and the others laughed and then one of them shouted, 'Off the boat, ye weirdy freak or we'll throw you off.'

I could make out who was who for the most part, a right gang of layabouts. Most of them were at my school and at least two from my village: Paddy Jack Boyle for one, fat pimply gouger that he was. 'Oh yeah, Paddy, ye great slab of pork, why don't you come and try.'

I wasn't that bothered for I didn't think any of them

would have the nerve to come out on to the boat. Sure it would be like them coming into your own home to have a crack at you. My bother would be me coming ashore and them waiting to clatter me when I got there.

There were four of them. Paddy you would hardly count, but there was a hard little fella from Blacksod, his name was Terence and his father was from Birmingham in England and he was always fighting. He couldn't speak Irish and he had had a hard time at the school to begin with on account of being English, though his mother was from that village all right. If I had to I could fight him, but I wouldn't do well if the others joined in.

'Get off the boat, Cormack and we'll let you live!' And with that the whole crew of them began to wade out. What the hell were they playing at? I didn't bother to answer them, of course. The way they were talking you'd think they came from some telly drama, it was that corny—but I looked about for something I could use in the way of a weapon. There was a short boat-hook, tucked in behind the wheel, so I unclipped that, rolled up my sleeves and stood waiting for them, and made sure they could see what I had in my hands and all, and that I meant business.

They looked fierce enough while they were wading, forging away, Terence, the little rat, pushing ahead of the others. If I could get a good crack in at him, I didn't think I'd have much trouble from the others.

When they were up close I gave them one more chance. 'You touch the boat, any one of you, and I swear I'll report you to the gardai and you'll be in heavy trouble.'

'Oh, and what are you doing there yourself, if it's not helping yourself to the pickings?'

'What are you talking about?' I really hadn't understood what they were up to at all.

'Listen,' said Terry, 'just because you people from Glosh think you're all great sailors doesn't mean to say we got to

144

listen to you, so get off that boat, and let us get on with our business.'

'Yeah,' said Paddy, eyeing my boat-hook and not looking as tough as he'd sounded when he was back on the beach. 'We could cut you in, Willie, if you like. My uncle said he could sell all the fittings we could bring him. What do you say?'

They were going to ravage the yacht!

'I told you,' I said quietly now, for I was feeling black angry, I can tell you, 'you put one fat finger on this boat and I'll crush it.'

'You git,' said Terry, and started to scrabble up the sloping side.

I didn't hesitate. I brought the boat-hook down right hard on the wrist of his right hand so that he cried out loud. I would have cracked him across the head to finish him off and maybe then I'd be up in Mountjoy prison with all the gangsters from Dublin for he would surely have died, but I didn't, I slipped and hit him on the shoulder. But it was enough, I can tell you. The little tyke. He yowled like a scorched cat and slithered back down into the water

'I'll get you,' he snarled, but he was in pain and his desperado pals could see that well enough and they weren't rushing to board the *Katya* now.

'You! And who else, your daddy?'

'Go on. If you all climb together he can't hurt you,' he said urging his gang on, but not one of them was convinced.

'It's not that important.'

'He can't stay out here all night.'

'Why bother. Come on, Terry.'

Gradually they cajoled him into accepting his and their temporary defeat, and it was temporary because I couldn't see myself stuck out here guarding the boat for a man who had disappeared on me. What had happened to him?

Slowly they sloshed back to the shore, one of them

holding Terry who, I'm happy to say, had hurt his leg it seemed when he had tumbled back down the boat's side. I was wise enough not to crow, nor even to answer them back when they hurled their final insults at me while wheeling their bikes off. I gave them five minutes, then I scrambled down the side and made to the shore. I walked up to the dry sand and then, making sure they weren't lurking somewhere up by the road, I sat down beneath the low dunes that edge the road to pull on my trainers.

'That was quite impressive for you, Willie Cormack.'

'Ian!' He was sitting up above me, tucked in some hollow, screened by the marram grass. 'How long have you been there?'

'Long enough.' He flicked the butt of the cigarette he'd been smoking out over my head so that it landed down beyond my feet.

'Is that right?' I stood up. 'A friend might have come to help,' I said curt enough, for certainly I would have helped him had he been stuck on his own.

'You weren't in any danger.'

That was easy enough to say. 'Thanks for letting me know.'

He shrugged. 'Anyway they were after the boat, not you, and I don't see why I should help that sod. He owes me money and besides he deserves getting paid back for what he did to Anna.'

'Oh, Christ, Ian, not you too. How in hell's name do you know what happened? Not even Anna could swear who came at her. I asked her and all she could say was that whoever it was has a mighty mark on his face from where she hit him.'

I let that sink in and then I said, 'You thought he was decent enough a while back. Don't you recall the night we all sat out here, and he and Anna danced on the strand. Are you telling me that you really think he would go round attacking someone, that man? If you do I swear you have less than no sense.'

'He owes me money.'

'Ah, belt up, will you.'

He laughed and slid down the dune to join me and he pulled out his smokes and lit another one and we talked, looking out at the sad yacht, and remembering the stormy night when Malouf blew in, and how everyone had gathered round to help, and now it was like everything had run into reverse. Ian didn't know and hadn't heard a thing as to where Malouf might be but he was interested to hear again what Anna had said about her attack.

'It was the right side of his face, was it?'

He asked me that a couple of times so that I was almost suspicious and checked to see that he himself wasn't sporting a bruise. He would only say that information was valuable and he had a few notions about the affair.

When I pressed him, he said he'd seen the Yank looking shifty as a rat, and he thought he'd seen Anna spending time with him the afternoon of the dance. Then he clammed up and would only agree that it might be worthwhile checking out Belmullet for Malouf. I also thought, given what Ian had said, that it would be worth tracking down the Yank. With any luck, he was the one sporting a bruise. And if that was the case I'd surely bust his fine American nose for him.

Ian laughed when I told him and said that I was in right danger of turning into Bruce Willis. I don't hold any faith in violence. Hate it. Hate it in the family. Hate it in the North. Hate it. But here I was, all ready to start throwing my weight around again.

'Lucky you're a skinny tyke,' he said, 'or else I might be worried.'

I grinned, pleased that he was still the Ian I'd always known and not just like all the other bowsers looking for trouble, and we went up on to the road and hitched a lift that took us right into Market Square. Ian said he would talk to the Yank first while I could do the round of the pubs to see if there was any sign of Malouf. I agreed.

Sixteen

There are some fellas my age, or younger even, that have to spend half their day scouring round the pubs looking for their old man. He'd be tucked away in a dark corner with a couple of drinking companions, nursing pints of the black stuff and he'd be forever swearing that he would be out there right away . . . That would be a kind of hell as far as I'm concerned. I'm happy enough out in Barratt's but that is maybe because I know everyone that's in there, but these pubs in the town were nothing to me. All of them seemed dark, all of them had knots of men, shoulders hunched over their drink talking quietly, and in all of them they would turn and look at me as I stood there at the door like I was from Mars or something; and in none of them was there sign nor word of Malouf.

'Never seen a black man in here?' A grizzled chin moved towards a pint glass.

'I did hear of him one time. A blackamoor, you say? Kind of a doctor, was he?'

The barman looked up. 'Maybe on market day, you would see one if you wanted . . . '

I went into every bar on the main street and then hurried back to Market Square where the New Royal Hotel stands, dominating the square and the town itself. I can remember the old hotel, at least the ruin of it, a tall, gaunt building, fine at one time, but sad and faded. Ah well, they took it down when they started to smarten the town up to bring in tourists and now they have this building with its swimming pool and expensive rooms.

Ian was by the front entrance, waiting for me. 'He was in his room,' he said. 'He's coming down to us.'

'That's very grand of him.'

'I thought so too.'

His car was in the car park the other side of the square and we were both surprised when one of the hotel staff came out with a couple of smart leather suitcases and carried them right over to the car and put them into the boot.

'Looks like our man is off,' remarked Ian.

It seemed that way and it made me all the more interested to see him, and particularly the state of his face.

'Well, boys. You wanted to have a word with me.' He was neat as a polished pin, all in smartly creased khaki, a soft leather jacket slung over his shoulder, and though the day didn't have that much blue in it, he was still wearing the sunglasses, like some movie star. 'I'm running kind of late. Got a plane in couple of hours.'

His face. Not a mark on it that I could see. I felt a flush of shame and glanced away.

Ian stepped in. 'Do you know anything about our African friend?'

'Nope. Jokey little guy, wasn't he? Got himself lost, huh?'

'Were you out at the village last night? Did you hear what happened to Anna?'

'The lovely Anna?' He stretched out the words as if they were a long strip of elastic. And was there any sign of concern? Not at all. He was looking over our shoulders and up the street. 'Is she all right? What happened? I left that shindig pretty early. Had a few words with your brother,' he said looking at me, 'then came right back here.'

'Someone attacked her last night.' I studied him, trying to read his reaction, the level of concern. 'In the dark. She didn't see who it was but . . . ' I hesitated, 'she left a mark on her attacker.'

'My God!' He put his hand to his glasses as if to take them off. 'That's terrible.'

Maybe I was wrong. He seemed shocked.

150

'She's all right. People are accusing Malouf.'

'That African guy. I see. That's maybe why he ran off, I guess. Police been told about it all?'

'Do you think they should?'

And the penny dropped with such a clang in my head, I thought my face would give it away. I bent down to do up my shoelace just to stop myself from lashing into him right there.

'Well, I guess I never like bringing in the cops unless . . . ' he let the sentence trail into the air, as he glanced towards his car. We were wasting his time.

'It wasn't the African, as you like to call him,' I snapped.

'Willie, we better be on our way.'

Maybe it was the anger in my voice he heard, for the Yank turned and studied me with sharper interest, his glasses black ice in the sunlight. 'Oh, is that right? Why're you so sure?'

'I know.'

He laughed. 'He's kind of excitable, wouldn't you say? Lived up at her house for a while, yeah? Know what I mean. Some of these fellas just expect women to come running 'cause that's the way they are . . . '

'Why would he beat her up? He wanted to marry her, for Chris' sakes!'

The answer came back smooth as grease. 'There you go,' he said, 'and I just bet she didn't want to marry him. Ain't that the picture? Excuse me now.' We stepped back out of his way.

''Fraid I cain't help you boys any more. My guess is your "friend" is halfway across the country by now, maybe heading for England, getting his butt right out of here. I wouldn't mind laying odds you won't be seeing him any more. Ain't that a shame.'

'I thought you were staying longer,' said Ian.

'Plans change.' And he walked off, pulling his car keys from his pocket, looking too smooth for Belmullet.

We watched him get in and then drive off, not taking the road for the airport but the one back up the Mullet. We looked at each other. 'What's his game?'

'Why did he keep his glasses on all the time?'

'Because he has a black eye?' suggested Ian.

'That's the truth.'

Ian looked surprised. 'You think so?'

'Certain.'

'Jesus!' Ian's face tightened into a mask; his fist clenched. 'Jesus, Willie! We should have killed him! Why didn't you say anything . . . ?'

'Calm down. You want to be like the laddoes last night, do you?'

'That filth!'

'Maybe, but without Anna's word there's no evidence against him, is there?' He looked blank at me. 'Is there?'

'He doesn't look like the kind of man who'd attack a girl, does he?'

'What do those kind of men look like?' I said.

We looked at each other. 'How are you so sure, Willie?'

'How did he know Malouf was missing? You never said he was, just asked what he knew about him.'

Ian nodded. 'Jeez, you're right, Willie. What do we do now?'

What could we do? 'Forget him,' I said. 'Mal is who we've got to find. Don't ask me why but I reckon Anna knows it was the Yank and all, and won't say anything.'

'Why?' He seemed hurt at the thought.

'I said don't ask me why. Listen. You phone Francis, see whether there's a boat missing. Maybe he's lit out as you suggested. I'll report him missing to the gardai. Meet you back here in ten minutes.'

The police were pleasant enough but the two of them that were in the office having tea seemed confident that nothing could have happened to Malouf. 'Sure, people don't disappear in this part of the world,' smiled the sergeant, 'unless they walk out into the sea.'

Of course.

I ran as fast as I could back out to Market Square and met Ian walking from the telephone box down by the post office. 'I think maybe he cracked and he drowned himself. Did you talk to Francis?'

'He's out with a party of anglers round Achill; won't be back till tomorrow. But there is another boat out. Mrs Deane saw it leaving about four this mornin'.'

'Do you think it was Mal?'

'It's possible.'

We had to get out to Blacksod as fast as we could. If he'd gone off on his own, we'd have to alert the authorities. God, there would be hell to pay, and everybody would then say for certain he was Anna's attacker. 'He's a blind eejit!'

'I don't know,' said Ian. 'I'm not sure he could manage to take out a boat on his own like that . . . You know, starting up, finding one with fuel . . . '

'He got here all the way from Africa.'

'Even so.'

We took a ride with a van and were out in the village by six-thirty. Then cycled on to Blacksod. There were no cars on the quay and when Ian scanned all the boats that are kept moored there, he was puzzled and so was I for there were none missing apart from Francis's.

We walked up to Mrs Deane's: she lives in one of the old lighthouse keeper's cottages and though she hardly steps out of her doorway she knows every whisper that takes place out there. She's all right though. She told us that the boat came back: Rob Macyntire's it was—he's a real bowser. One of the no-gooders after Malouf the night before. A heavy-set, dark-jowled fisherman who always seemed to have hard looking cousins from Birmingham staying with him in the salmon season. The odd thing was, and she couldn't swear to this, but she thought my brother, John James, had been out with him.

'Him!' Ian and I looked at each other. 'He has no interest in fishing.'

'Just the two of them was it, Mrs?' said Ian.

She leaned forward all conspiratorial. 'Not at all,' she said. There'd been a sort of bundle of men getting out of the car, so she hadn't noted many of the faces. Funny thing was, one fella seemed to have drink taken for there were a couple of them holding him up. Why they would want to take an auld drunkard out she couldn't tell.

'Was it the African?'

Her face closed up. 'Couldn't tell,' she repeated.

'Better if Malo had gone off on his own,' said Ian.

'We can't be sure he was with them.'

We walked slowly back out to the quay. It was bad whichever way you looked at it, it was a bad business. And John with them . . . Why would John James be out on a boat at that hour in the morning and his friend, the Yank, sliding off and with him maybe sporting a black eye under those fancy dark glasses . . . ?

Ian was looking out to Duvillaun, glancing up at the sky and then wandering over to the edge of the quay, making some kind of calculation about the tide or the wind.

'Even a blind goose would know Malo was innocent.'

'Aye.'

'Except,' I said, 'if he ran off or disappeared maybe. Then sure he would look guilty.'

'And there would be no harm to the Yank, so long as Anna kept quiet.'

'That's what I was thinking.'

'If you wanted to get rid of someone where would you dump them?'

'In the sea . . . '

'And if you didn't want to commit murder?'

'On the Inishkeas?'

'I'd say so.'

'And do you think my brother was in with them?'

He didn't answer.

'I can't believe John was on that boat at all. God knows he can be rough, Ian, but this would be cold blooded . . . ' I couldn't bring myself to voice what we both knew it was.

Ian pulled a face and spat over the edge of the quay into the water. 'I saw him thick with Rob Macyntire in the pub. He had business with him, I'm sure of that.'

'Will we confront Macyntire then?'

'Are you soft! He'd slaughter us. I have a better idea, Will. Look here.'

I went over to where he was standing and looked down. The sea was calm enough here on this side of the bay but there was nothing alongside the quay but a curragh with two pairs of oars shipped in it. 'There's the race in a fortnight,' he said. He tipped his head on one side. 'It's not a bad curragh. Macyntire's, I believe.'

'Are you mad! I know what you're thinking. You're daft! We'd not make it halfway to the islands in that . . '

'If we time it right we would have the tide running with us both ways.'

'Not in a million years . . . '

'If they took him out to the islands, what kind of shape do you think he's in, Willie? Maybe a broken leg, maybe a broken back. Maybe they dumped him over the side and we'll never find him, but can you rightly live with yourself if we don't find out, can you? And who's there to ask to take us out. Francis might have listened, TJ too, but his boat is up on dry dock; the rest would think we're cracked.'

'But it's not possible to row that far.'

'Five mile. And you know it's possible, and in worse seas than this.'

I knew what he meant. My poor father had managed it on the night of the storm. And the funny thing was that the only request he'd made of me lying there in that hospital bed was to go out to the islands and find his godstone. I hadn't put much thought to it, to be honest. Well, perhaps this was the time and I felt a sickness in my gut as I began to realize what I was letting myself in for. 'What do you know about the godstone, Ian?'

'Why?'

And I told him the strange thing my father had said to me back in the hospital.

'You come out in that curragh, Will Cormack, and I swear I'll go and dive in that sound, if it's at all possible, and look for the stone for ye.'

And so we agreed we'd set out the next morning. Five miles, I said to myself, is not so far. But looking back I think it is far enough to change your whole life.

We shook hands.

We said nothing to anyone and next morning we were back at the quay, the curragh bobbing lightly on the water just beneath where we were standing.

'Are you set?' said Ian.

'I am.'

'Good man,' said Ian and grinned. He loved this. Sure, to him it was a mighty crack. And then a thought struck him. 'Wait up,' he said and sprinted off towards the road, leaping down on to the sand, cutting the corner to save time. He ran straight to a little lock-up shed where the fishermen kept gear. A moment later he came struggling back into view, an outboard in one hand and a can of fuel in the other. I ran to give him a hand.

'What do you say? Better than oars, eh?'

'Whose is it?'

'Macyntire's.'

'He'll kill us if he finds out.'

Ian laughed. 'In for a penny. He'll kill us for taking the boat anyhow. Don't worry, we'll be back well before night.'

'God willing.'

Seventeen

I sat on the centre thwart and kept my eyes fixed dead ahead and said not a word while we motored round past Falmore and the bust-up pier at Surge View. The ocean here can crack and wear and hurl solid concrete from where it has been rightfully set until nothing remains, and after only a short number of years too; but I didn't think of that.

We rode past Duvillaun Island, which is like a green shoulder heaved out of the sea, right at the wide entrance to Blacksod Bay. No one has lived on that island for long years though my father always said there was good grazing for sheep there. And then we were out in the wide ocean and I could see the Inishkeas before us.

Neither of us had spoken since setting off. I wouldn't say Ian was the most sensitive person on the Mullet but he knew well enough to let me alone, but now with the mainland well behind us, he said, 'Ye're OK, Willie, yeah?'

I glanced back at him: like a little lord at ease with the world, his world, not mine, one hand on the gunwale, the other on the handle of the outboard, leaning back into the corner of the aft thwart with his legs stretched out before him, the wind ruffling his red hair and a happy smile on his face. Jesus, I did envy him, that's the truth. 'I'm all right,' I said.

'Good man.'

And the miracle was that I was too. I think maybe it was seeing the islands and knowing that after all this time I was truly going to set foot on them. Certainly I thought of Malouf and hoped we would find some sight or sign of him but in my heart I feared this was unlikely. If some hard men, and

I included John in that, had snaffled him up and taken him out in a fishing boat, they would hardly have given him a pleasure cruise to the islands. More likely they had fed him to the sea.

I pushed that thought from my mind.

You think the ocean is empty but that is not so. I don't mean all the life beneath the surface but above. I saw birds, gulls wheeling around us and short black and white birds— Ian said they were guillemots—that bobbed on the surface and then ducked down, diving when we came close. I looked and saw terns arrowing into the waves, and one coming up beside us that close that I could see the little fish wriggling in its beak. And a black-back gull, like some grizzled pirate, harrying it from one side, then the other, trying to get it to drop its catch, which it did, making the tern scream in anger.

There was a stiff breeze running behind us, flicking the tops of the waves into white. But the sun was shining and the sea was a crisp green and we sped along, slapping over the top of the water like a skimming stone. Perhaps I caught something of Ian's excitement, for that scrap of a tune I was working on came to me as I sat there looking ahead to the south island, still and solid and solitary. It was still a tune with no words and only three parts complete, but it hummed in my head.

'Not long now.'

And it wasn't either before we were motoring towards the broad quay my father had described so often, and the white sandy cove off to the left. And then we were suddenly in sheltered water, and Ian throttled back on the engine, and we puttered round the quay that had been built to last for many a lifetime.

To the right of the harbour was Rusheen Island, which, now I could see it up close, was hardly an island at all for there was barely any water between it and the shore, even

159

at this height of the tide. There was nothing on it but a few bits of old iron from the boilers to tell of the whaling business that went on there. And then, lining all that sandy beach between pier and island, were the houses of my father's family and relations and friends, all silent. Though the sunlight made them gleam, this close they looked sad, all the white washed from them, all the doors closed and rotted at the heels. Many of the roofs were gone, or had slates missing, all the chimneys were cracked and not one was threading smoke to suggest life.

We found him. That was the second miracle of the day.

After we'd tied up the curragh at the quay, we began to check all the ruined houses, one after the other. There was only one that was weather tight—a cabin some naturalist had put up. So he could study the geese, Ian said, when they flew in at the back end of the winter. There were heavy shutters on the windows of the cabin and a fine big lock on the door—and no sign of Malouf.

We shouted and called out but there was no answer, only the crying of the birds.

We had worked our way along the fifteen or so houses that line the foreshore and were about to turn back to check the ten or so that formed a ragged second line, for that was all the number of households that had ever been in it, when we came to the last and biggest of the houses and more of a ruin than any of the others, it was too. It had been a school, Ian said. The door had long gone; there was no glass nor board in the window, nor any bit of roof, only the four walls, rising up high at the gable ends.

Ian had already started to walk back when something, I don't know what, made me turn in at the doorway. Weed and grass had grown up through the stone floor so that it was like a wild garden in there; and there he was, curled up in the corner by the dead fireplace, looking dead himself too.

He'd no shoes—how pale and bony his feet looked—nor a coat of any kind. Hadn't he been wearing my coat when we ran through the black storm? I couldn't remember.

'Ian!'

I took a step closer, nervous I suppose, fearing a dead man. His eyes I could see now were open, his thin face not that shiny black he had but almost grey, and sure to God that is the colour of death. He'd a dark swollen patch where he'd been clattered high up on the jaw, and his mouth was puffed and the lip broken. Poor fella, I thought, you're a long way from your mountains now.

'They beat him,' I said, 'before dumping him here for dead.'

'I pinned my hopes on that man,' Ian murmured. It wasn't bitter the way he said it, but kind of surprised. Indeed, looking at Malouf now, a piece of flotsam washed into the ruins by a high tide, you couldn't ever imagine how he could have made us believe in his dream of the fine life he would be having in Germany.

'We'd better move him,' I said.

'Aye.'

I went to lift him by the shoulders and it was only then that I had the shock of my life. It was like he was shivering deep inside. I pulled him over on to his back so suddenly that Ian exclaimed at my roughness.

'Mind it, Willie! What are you—?'

I laid my head on his chest listening for a heartbeat. Very faint it was, and that was the third miracle.

But he was cold, not an ounce of warmth in him at all. I fell to rubbing his hands. 'Do the same to his feet,' I said, 'hard as ye can.' I stripped off my jumper and wrapped it round him and Ian did the same. But after a few minutes of this and not a stir out of your man, Ian sat back on his haunches.

'This is no good. We have to get him properly warm. He'll not make it back alive otherwise.'

I agreed but what could we do? The place was one big graveyard—nothing to bring back a man half drowned and bitter frozen to the soul.

'I know,' said Ian. 'Lift him up there. We'll take him to that cabin.'

'Break in?'

'Why not?'

I took one side and he the other and so we hoisted Malouf between us, not that he carried much weight at all, and trailed him back along the sandy shore in front of all those silent houses, back to the quay. Then for the second time struck up a narrow slip of a track past a tumbled cottage.

We laid Malouf gently in the sun and out of the wind, and studied how to crack our way into this nut.

The padlock was too hefty to force without an iron bar, which we did not have. 'So it's in through the window then,' said Ian. He produced his knife and worked away at the hinges of the shutter for a couple of minutes and then called me over to take the weight of one side and between us we lifted the thing down. Then we busted the glass out of the window.

Being the smaller of the two of us Ian undid the catch and slipped through, rooted around till he found a bag of tools, then scrambled out, cut through the padlock and then we were in properly.

The inside was done up snug enough, all pine wall and ceiling, and a standing stove with turf all ready, and a cooking stove. We set to work and soon had a fire, and a can of soup simmering on the stove. We stripped Malouf, wiped him down with a towel for he was clammy with damp or cold sweat, and then wrapped him in blankets. We tried to feed him a bit of soup, which he took, though he still hadn't made any sign of seeing or hearing anything

162

that was happening around him. Then we laid him by the stove, hoping that the soup and the heat would bring him back to himself.

After that there was little we could do for him, so we left him there and went out to check the curragh.

The boat was fine, floating on no more than six inches of water for the tide had run out in the time we had been there, but the outboard, when Ian peered into its little tank, was low on fuel.

'Have we enough to get back?' I asked. 'The mainland looks so close. See, I can make out our houses. Would you believe it?'

'We're close, but not close enough.' He glanced up at the sky. 'The wind is shifting round which will help. If we wait a while, which we have to anyway because of our man in there, we'll have the tide running our way too. Then I reckon we might have enough to get halfway.'

'You're not serious!'

He smiled. I don't think anything bothered Ian when it came to boats, and more than that I reckon he enjoyed having the upper hand on me this while. 'You told me yourself that your rowing skills were mightily improved.'

'And so they are. But . . . '

'But nothing. There are two pair of oars; and I tell you, there's no other way of getting home, Willie, unless you can whistle up the sea fairies.'

I looked out at that sea and imagined what it must have looked like when my father and all the other men of the island had set out in their curraghs after the salmon, so many black beetles on the water, and then the storm hitting them. Why had only two boats made it safely? There must have been some ill luck on them all.

Then I remembered what my father had said to me when I had visited him in the hospital: if only you could raise the godstone then all the luck of the islands would come back. I reminded Ian of this.

'We could do with a bag of luck,' he said.

There were three old cormorants stuck on the end of the quay, their wings stretched out to dry. I have heard stories that they're not real birds at all but poor drowned sailors who can't fly to heaven.

'Do ye have any idea where the stone was tossed?'

'Sure, Dad told me. Up by the channel between the islands.'

It was easy enough to find the place he had described, right at the closest point between the two islands, and even the little natural ledge of flat rock from which he'd said the priest had made the islanders swing it, one, two, three and out into the deep water.

I never realized how close the two islands were. Here it was only too easy to imagine them shouting angry words at each other and hurling stones. Madness to live that close and not get on, so I thought, but maybe people need a difference to fight against; maybe, I thought, it made them feel stronger in themselves. I could see a kind of sense in it perhaps.

We stood on the rim of the channel looking down into the crystal clear water. It didn't look that deep; you could see stone and strands of weed waving slackly up at us.

'Not deep? You're joking. Maybe twenty foot and dangerous.'

'Could you dive down?'

'I could, and I suppose this would be the best time when the tide is out and hasn't started to run yet. It's dangerous, mind.'

'You wouldn't do it if it were that dangerous,' I said.

He grinned. 'Well, do you reckon you can row the curragh back on your own if anything happens to me?'

'If anything happens to you, I'd be that cross that I'd

jump in after you to make sure that you were truly drowned and not just pretending.'

'What's she look like then?'

I described the stone as exactly as I could. It was shiny black and sort of in the shape of a head. You could see the eyes and a nose. It would be too big for any man to lift on his own but even to locate it would be a fine thing, and sure, once it was found we could organize a right expedition to have it brought up.

He dived three times and finally scrambled up exhausted and frozen. It was too hard to get right down, he said, and you would need right diving gear to really look properly. I took it for a bad sign for our return journey, though I held my tongue, for it would only anger Ian to hear me say as much.

When we got back Malouf was in better shape. He didn't sit up when we came in but his eyes were focused. 'Two thief,' he whispered, his voice so hoarse you would think the water had turned the inside of his throat to rust.

'We thought you were a dead man.' said Ian

'Dead,' Malouf repeated in that hoarse whisper, 'I was dead.' Then he closed his eyes.

Ian went over to the door and looked out.

I felt Malouf's forehead—still clammy and cold, but some of that dreadful greyness had faded. There was no doubt he would mend if we could get him back home and into a warm, dry bed, but would he survive the journey back? I voiced these thoughts to Ian who shook his head and said now was our best chance for he didn't like the look of the sky, and if the weather fully broke we could be stuck out on the island for days. So there was nothing for it but to tidy up, clean out the stove, put back the shutter and then ease Malouf up on to his feet and take him down to the curragh.

He still hadn't the strength to walk but at least he wasn't dragging his feet like a corpse. He even protested faintly that he could stand unaided when we were trying to get him down into the boat, but when I let him go he swayed so badly that I had to grab him before he nose-dived into the water. I sat him down on the edge and then Ian took his legs and together we eased him into the stern, wrapped and wedged in the blankets we'd borrowed from the house. Ian started the engine, then I cast off and jumped into the bows and we puttered out of that silent harbour with only the row of lonely houses to witness our departure.

Ian had been right to wait, for the wind had backed into the north-west and so would help to blow us home. But the sky looked awfully dark behind us. When I pointed this out to him, he just said, 'It will be rough.'

It was.

Within ten minutes we had lost the shelter that the Inishkeas gave us and the sea first dipped and swelled, then grew steep and angry, and the outboard howled as the stern was lifted high out of the water. Sometimes it felt as if we were sliding backwards and then sometimes as if we were almost flying on the breaking crest of a wave, the white water bubbling behind us.

I tucked myself down into the bows, and scooped at the water slopping about in the belly of the curragh with the bailer. Better to concentrate on that rather than the sea around us. Malouf looked like a garden gnome, in bad need of a coat of paint. His eyes were closed but his lips were moving, maybe in prayer. Ian looked serious, all the time judging the size of the following wave and how best to take it. Nobody spoke.

An old gull drifted over us, then suddenly wheeled away with a loud skreeling cry, and let the wind carry it high up and away. The sky darkened but the coast, rimmed clearly with white, was still visible.

When we were almost midway, the engine sputtered and then died. Ian quickly twisted the cap off the tank and peered inside. 'She's finished now. Out with the oars, Will.'

I didn't pause to think that all of this was the stuff of my worst dreams, I just did what I was told, anxious to keep us moving; for merely to drift on that kind of a sea, beam on to a breaking wave, and we'd have been rolled over easy as a barrel of beer.

'Pull hard with the right,' Ian shouted, and I did. 'Now both and keep it steady.' I pulled, trying to get a rhythm I could keep to. The oars of a curragh are crude, heavy things, with not much of a blade at the end, and held by one wooden pin. Ian lashed rope round the engine and then took the middle thwart and unshipped his own oars. 'Keep time with me,' he said.

Now there was only the creak of the oars, the hissing of the waves and the sound of the wind. We seemed to row for ever and my hands were raw and my back and neck ached like the devil, and every time I looked over my shoulder the coastline seemed darker and no nearer. Malouf's eyes were open and there was a ghost of a smile on his face. His mouth moved. 'Is he saying something?' I shouted to Ian.

'He says,' said Ian over his shoulder, 'that in the desert no one drowns.'

'That's a comfort,' I said. 'Now that he's awake, does he have anything else useful to tell us?'

Ian passed on my message and I saw Malouf lift his head and look round Ian to me. Again I couldn't hear him and again Ian passed on what he said. 'The fella is truly gone in the head,' he said.

'Why's that?' Behind me I could hear the dull crumbling roar of breaking surf.

'He says that they will not let us drown.'

'Who's they?'

167

'All the men.' He paused, resting on his oars and I followed likewise. 'All the poor sods already drowned.'

'I hope he's right.'

'Me too.'

In my dream the hands were reaching out of the water to pull me down, down into the dark, that's what I always felt.

It is a wonder how we kept going. I suppose both Ian and I were tougher than I ever thought. We would pull for fifteen or twenty minutes and then have a short rest, then pull again. Malouf stirred himself out of his blanket and bailed, singing away to himself, bits of which I could hear to begin with. But with the rising wind and the building sound of the surf on the coast, even Ian's shouted commands were whipped away.

I don't know what the time was, maybe ten, ten-thirty and the light was all but gone. The breakers roared ahead of us now and I was so tired that I could neither think or worry, I just hurt. I didn't care what happened, only that we would come to an end, and sooner rather than later.

'Steady, Will.'

I rested on my oars.

Ian turned round to me. 'Maybe they have seen us. We are going to try for the north end of Glosh beach.'

I nodded at him.

It's a dangerous strand where nobody swims. There's a ripping undertow and the sand shelves into a wall that the waves smack into. If we got as far as that without capsizing we would surely be broken in two. Still, the north end was a little softer. I minded that the waves were more broken up there for some reason, and the beach shelved more gently.

'Pull now.'

We pulled. And paused. Coming closer and closer. 'Now.' And again.

I watched a wave building behind us, higher and higher it grew, curling like a hand to reach out and smash down on us. 'Now!'

This was the one. We pulled, heaving at the oars. One. Two. Dip. Pull. Out. One. Two. Dip. Pull. Up went the stern. 'Stop!' Ian yelled, and almost in one movement he flipped one of his oars off the pin, lifted the other high over his head and, shifting himself back into the stern beside Malouf, smacked the oar down beside the outboard, forcing it into the now breaking face of the wave. The last sight I had of him was his face stretched in a battle yell, his legs braced against the centre thwart, and both arms straining at the oar. Malouf was leant up against him, adding his weight on to the oar, trying to give us steerage, so that we weren't flipped high like a coin.

The wave roared around us and over us, my oars were ripped away, something thwacked me hard in the chest, and then all was white freezing sea, and tumbling, my lungs bursting to break out of my chest, and salt, and I was fighting a thousand devils it seemed. Something banged into my side. I thought my hand touched sea bottom, sand . . . I scrabbled for a second, and my head burst out of the water and I sucked air and then was down again and then up, and then, feeling sure that this was it, for there was no strength, none at all left in me, and that treacherous undertow was stripping me back out of my depth. Then all of a sudden I felt a hand tighten on my own, firm, hard, steadying me.

Slowly, step by step, I came on to the shore, and then the hand was gone and I was down on my knees with the water tumbling me towards the beach, and then sucking me right back out again, as if all the time it wanted me back into its reach. Then there were people around me and I felt myself being half lifted, half carried up on to the shore.

Eighteen

I heard Brede and Gary shouting and saw figures in the surf.

'Oh, dear God! Oh, sweet Jesus!'

Brede, dry and tough as marram grass, sounded as if her heart was breaking.

'Ian!'

I never thought she cared for him that much. You know, loved him.

I wanted to get up and go to her but my legs wouldn't move from under me. Someone threw a blanket round my shoulders and when I shifted my arm to pull it tighter I felt a sharp stab in my rib. Funny what you are aware of and what you notice when something terrible is happening.

Sure you cannot drown in the desert but the sea between here and Inishkea is full of drowned men. It was a miracle, the fourth, that I had survived and no surprise that of Ian and Malouf there was no sign.

Something long and black rolled in on a high breaking wave.

I heard Gary yell, 'Look out!' and then the curragh, or what was left of it, thundered down on to the sand.

There was the sucking drag of the sea pulling out, snatching at the legs of the men in the water and then, for some reason, I looked left, down to the really wicked part of the beach. I saw lights, and a car pulling up—turned out to be Patrick Brannagh, a young garda from Belmullet, and Rob Macyntire the owner of the curragh. But I'll tell you about that in a while, for I mean to get the events as straight as I can. And as that car turned, its lights swept down on to the strand, and there, by the grace of God, was Ian out in the surf. How, I don't know, but there he was and not alone either, for he had his arm round our Malouf.

I screamed my head off. 'Brede!'

She turned, and saw, and then with the others she started to run.

I did get up and saw Ian disappear again, and then there they were the two of them, Ian on his knees this time and a little further out. Then Gary it was ran in and grabbed first one and then the other, and dragged them up out of the sea's reach. He is that strong, Gary. I was raging because I couldn't move and I didn't know whether the two of them were truly all right and no one seemed to be coming to me, though of course someone did—Mick Barratt it was who hoisted me right up and brought me to the track where the cars were.

That was the first part of it.

You'd think there might be some kind of jubilation that we'd all made it safe. But not a bit of it. No heroes' welcome at all. Gary called me a right eejit and, when he saw that I wasn't bad hurt, cuffed me round the head. But that was nothing to what Robbie Macyntire said. It was he who'd called the gardai. He wanted us arrested! He did.

He shoved Brede out of the way and grabbed Ian by the scruff of his neck. 'Ye thieving little blackguard,' he shouted. 'That engine cost three hundred quid and I swear you'll pay me every penny of it back, plus what I've lost from not being able to go fishing. What do you say?' Then he seemed to notice Malouf, a little behind Ian, and just for a moment I thought he looked startled. Then he shook his fist and the anger was in his voice, as thick as raw meat. 'I'll have your guts too. And the black fella!'

Malouf was leaning forward, cradling his left arm which seemed to be hanging kind of awkward. He looked up at this and stared full at Macyntire, his eyes large and white in that

171

darkness, not a trace of fear in him though. 'You,' he said speaking with some difficulty, though I heard him and so did Macyntire, 'you were one of the men.' I didn't know what he meant by that.

Perhaps Macyntire did, though, for he spat on the sand and took a step forward, ignoring Ian now. 'I reckon we should toss this black freak back into the sea. That's what I reckon. What do you say, lads?'

He is the sort of man who always has two or three butties at his shoulder, heavy men, murmuring their agreement, squaring themselves up behind him. Maybe young Pat Brannagh would have put a stop to him but he was still up at the garda car.

'You're right, Robbie, throw the tyke back.'

Gary laughed, in disbelief. 'Leave it, Rob.'

'Keep out of this, Cormack. And keep your wee brother out of my way from now on.'

I'm sure it was mainly talk and would never have amounted to anything for there was Brannagh on his way down, a heavy torch swinging in his hand. Though Gary had taken a step back I think he must have thought the man was only threatening, but I tell you who didn't step back and that was Brede.

Have you ever seen a small dog, a terrier maybe, turning on a couple of bigger dogs that have been hassling it? That was Brede. God, she was mighty! I swear she rolled up her shirt sleeves right in front of that man, and roared at him: 'Who do you think you are, you little scut of a rat, Robert Macyntire. You were always a sneaking and snivelling misery of a child, and you're worse now that you're fat. Get out of here before I have that man there,' pointing to Pat Brannagh who was now on us, his fresh face looking a bit stunned in a vacant sort of way, 'arrest you for threatening behaviour.'

'Aye,' said Gary standing beside her.

Suddenly I was aware of others, Mick Barratt, Danny Gilvoy from Glosh, Eddie, and more besides who must have come on to the beach in ones and twos as word of the action spread. Just drawing in, natural and easy, behind Brede, like a comforting and protective wall, and I felt a warmth in me that had all but died the night when Mal and I had run from the drunks.

Macyntire tried to bluff it out.

'Out of the way, Mrs—'

'Don't you Mrs me,' and she took a step forward and swung a hard closed fist smack into his cheek. And that finally spurred Brannagh into action.

'That'll do,' he said, pushing in front of Macyntire. I'm not sure whether it was to protect him or Brede because I wouldn't have put it past that man to raise his hand against a woman. 'Move back now, all of you, and we'll have the lads out of here.'

'My boat!'

'We can sort that out later.'

'I want—'

' "I want" nothing!' There was the full voice of the law settling in now. 'Any trouble from you, Robbie, and I'll charge you.'

Macyntire backed off muttering angrily to his butties, then turned and the three of them walked up to their car. There was some laughter at his retreat too. The beam of their lights swept over us as they turned, and then drove away.

'And where did you learn to box like that, Brede?' said Gary.

'Well, it wasn't in church,' said Brede shortly.

I saw Malouf being lifted up, and someone giving Ian a hand. Brannagh asked me a few questions but all I could tell him was that we'd been looking for Malouf who'd gone missing and we had feared that he was drowned but that we had found him on the island and half dead too.

Brannagh shook his head, a bit like a calf being bothered by flies, I thought, obviously not able to take in the half of what I was trying to tell him. Then Brede hooshed him off and told him he could ask as many questions as he liked the next day for not one of us would be going anywhere at all.

She gave me a searching look while I was being helped to my feet. 'Cracked a rib, have you?'

'Reckon I have.'

'Your mother will be worried sick.'

I let that pass.

'I thought you had more sense than to go rarin' about on the ocean with my Ian.'

'Could hardly let him go on his own, could I?'

Her tough face softened for a moment, then without another word to me she turned and hurried after Ian and Malouf. 'Both back to my house,' I heard her saying.

Gary walked with me back home and Mary and my mother were up and waiting. Mary hugged me till I yelped with the hurt in my chest. My mother bustled about and was that nervous that after she'd made us both hot soup, she burst into tears. I have only seen her cry one time before when I was very young and my father was still fishing and he was back one day late. I think that was the time he gave up the fishing altogether. She dabbed her face and patted my cheek and told me I was wicked. I reckoned she must have been worrying about my father.

I slept in my own room that night, with Gary in the other bed. There was no word of John James and I didn't think to ask but I did thank Gary and I said that our mother was not like her usual self.

'Didn't you know that the one thing that gives her a holy terror is the sea, Willie? Didn't you know that? She stopped Dad and it broke his heart to agree, but agree he did. She never let me, nor John, out in the boats. We always thought she had given you her fear but after tonight,' he said with a smile, 'I would say we were wrong. I saw you at the oars before she went up and over. You looked the proper sailor.'

'You're all talk,' I said.

But I had never known that about my mother. It was some wonder she even agreed to live right here in Glosh with the Atlantic breathing down her neck all the weeks of the year.

No wonder there was some distance between herself and the old fella. How was it that they ever got together except that she must have loved him fiercely, and he her if he gave up the sea, for it also meant not going back to his island.

I think I was asleep before my head hit the pillow.

Nineteen

You know how one day is much like any other, the little routines, who does what, where people sit, the jobs, all that. The pattern is always the same; the way people treat you and you look at them. And none of that ever changes. Yet when I opened my eyes the morning after Ian and I brought Malouf back in the curragh from the Inishkeas everything was different.

I felt it in myself to start with, and I don't mean the crack in my rib that pinched me when I breathed hard. Nor that Gary's bed was empty and made up and from the look of the sky half the day had gone; I mean I felt older, that I had passed some corner.

I heard quiet voices in the kitchen and slowly got myself up and dressed, all the while looking out of the window. What a deceiver that ocean is, for from where I stood, it looked so blue and calm that you'd never imagine how just that little while ago it'd been tearing and breaking like a seething wild thing. I knew also that what I was seeing then was not how it really was, for if I went on a boat it would not be quite so soft and calm at all. Odd the way that thought, going out on a boat I mean, didn't bother me.

My mother tried to make me go back to bed and wait on the doctor but there was too much I had to do, and I said I would not. To my surprise there was no argument from her. She made me sit where she always put John, by the window, and brought me tea and rashers and eggs, and once I started to eat I found I was desperate hungry.

I asked where John was but she said she didn't know. Then she snapped at Mary who had been out hanging clothes on the line, for no good reason. Mary just made a sign for me to say nothing and went out herself while my mother swept the floor so aggressively I thought she might take half an inch off the tiles. I didn't care about him any road. If John was gone so much the better, that's what I reckoned.

I ate in silence while she cleaned around me. Then, sitting down at the table opposite, she told me that Ian was up and about but there was no sign of the darkie. She couldn't see why Brede had taken him in, she said, but it was like her to be contrary in all things. I think she would have gone on but I told her that it was a kindness in Brede to look after the man when no one else would and that more than that he was my friend and I thought it only right that she should call him by his right name. She did not answer me one way or the other but I minded that the next time she referred to him it was as 'that Malouf fella', which was fair enough.

Gary came in from moving the cattle—my job—washed up, and then started to bustle my mother and Mary into getting ready, for he was to drive them into town to see Dad, who was doing a wee bit better apparently.

He's all noise, Gary, but decent. I went out to the bathroom and stood by the door while he sloshed water over his head and face and scrubbed his hands. When I tried to thank him he would have none of it. 'If I didn't like your fiddle playing so much, I would never have bothered at all.'

'I'll write a tune for you,' I said.

'You're soft in the head! What would I do with a tune named after me?'

But I will and I will play it in Barratt's if I get the chance, before he goes back to England. I even know that it will be a rough sort of a jig. I have the bones of it in my head right now.

My mother wouldn't have me come with them, she said I wasn't fit. The next day would do and she looked at me as she said this as if half expecting me to disagree, but I did not for my rib was sore enough. Though I wanted to see my

177

father and tell him everything. I did not want to be wincing while I was in there, and I also wanted to talk to him on his own without the family hanging on to what we were saying.

When Mary was getting in the car, my mother held back, fiddling with the bag she had with her. 'Willie,' she said, 'you have to promise me one thing now.'

'What's that?'

'Not to go out in the boats again.'

I was taken aback by the way she asked me, soft, you know, almost hesitant, like she was nervous I might say no to her. When I stopped and thought about what she was asking I knew that that was exactly what I would have to say and I was sorry that I had to deny her this thing.

'No,' I said, 'I cannot promise you that. So never ask me again.'

'Your father gave me his word on it for himself.'

I looked at her straight. 'I am not my father,' I said, 'nor anyone else in this family.'

She lifted her head and I caught the surprised look in her eyes. She blinked rapidly. 'True, you are your own man, William, but sometimes you seem to have little sense in your head, though the school is forever telling me that you have a brain.'

Gary sounded the horn.

'I thought it was a mad and foolish thing you and that Ian did yesterday, but perhaps you had to do it all the same.'

'Aye, we did. No word from the gardai is there?'

'No. No doubt you'll have some story to tell them.'

'Only the truth.'

She gave a quick smile. 'God bless,' she said, and was gone.

I immediately struck up the lane towards Brede's for I wanted to see Ian and Malouf. I knew that we had to sort ourselves out about the curragh and motor we had borrowed, and would not be returning, for I surely didn't want to have to face Macyntire some dark night and get a beating from him. But before I got to her gate, there was a shout from up the road and then careening down the hill on an old rattletrap black bike was Ailish King.

'Hey, Willie!' she shouted. 'Wait up there a minute.'

So I waited for her, half watching a couple of crows flapping and wheeling round the tower. They were always there and ugly though they were, I liked them.

Ailish King was in my class at school from day one. Always sitting at the side. Wild and quick so that you never knew what she was at for she was that changeable—like the wind. The teachers were wary of her and so were we boys because she had a sharp tongue and eyes that would flame out at you. Slight, skinny almost, and dark. Not raven like Anna but dark all the same, brown, and not wiry like some, but soft.

She was often round at Anna's house for though Anna was a couple of years older they were cousins and strangely enough Ailish used to mind Anna's little brothers. She was good with the very young.

'How're you?' I said as she pulled up and rested one foot on the ground and the other on the pedal. 'Have you come to see Ian?' That was a joke. She and Ian mainly fought with each other. She would needle him and not being a great man for the quick word, he would lash out.

'No.' She was a little out of breath. I couldn't help thinking that she had grown up more than I thought. She was quite the young woman now. 'Messages for Brede.' She indicated a little bag she had slung over her shoulder. There didn't look to me as if there was much in it.

'She's maybe up at the house. Are you going to go up or do you want me to take them for you, for I want to go in myself.'

' 'Tis all right.' She made no move to get off her bike. 'I was there when you came in last night,' she said. 'Are you all right.'

'Reckon so.'

'It must have been great crack.'

I couldn't help smiling at that. Wasn't it just like her to think being tossed about and near drowned as a crack. 'I don't know,' I said. 'Maybe you would have fancied it, Ailish, but I'm not certain I would go through it again unless I had to.'

She smiled too. 'Will you be well enough to play at the dance?'

There was a big do in a fortnight, after the races and sports and all. I reckoned I would be fit to play, not that I had been asked to yet.

'And if I ask you?' she said.

'I don't believe I would have the courage to say no,' I said. 'For you would terrify a judge.'

'Will Cormack, I've a mind to brain you for that.' But she made no attempt to do so, I am pleased to say, for in the state I was in she would surely have had the better of me. 'Anna's off to America,' she said. 'Did you hear that?'

That was a piece of news all right! 'Just like that?'

She seemed to be looking at me keenly. 'Yes,' she said, careless, you know, like 'so what'.

'How did she get the money? And what about the fella who attacked her, has that been sorted . . . '

She shrugged. 'She told me that the Yank paid the fare. Brendan Ballantine, has a great ring to it that name, doesn't it? Did you like him?'

I shook my head.

'Me neither. Not my type. Apparently he set her up with a fine, fancy job in Chicago. She's over the moon.'

'She's in love with Ballantine, is she?'

Ailish pursed her lips and shook her head. 'That's the odd thing—she won't talk about him at all.'

That didn't surprise me, not if he was the one who'd tried to assault her. It seems our Anna was made of tough material and it even crossed my mind, though I said nothing of it to Ailish, that maybe Anna had been making a bit of hay out of this. Blackmail? I didn't care one way or the other. 'And she's said nothing about the night she was set on.'

'Not a word,' said Ailish. 'Strange, I would howl the place down if it'd been me.'

'No one would attack you, Ailish, unless they weren't the full shilling.'

'Oh. Am I ugly then?'

'Don't be daft.'

'You fancied Anna, didn't you?'

And I heard the dry barking call of one of the crows, like a mocking echo, as it passed over us.

'Not really,' I said.

'Liar. She told me you followed her round like a pup. And I seen you myself. Didn't she even teach you to row in a curragh and you who wouldn't even dip your toe near the water, unless she asked you.'

'Well, I don't fancy her now.' And I didn't. The love I had or thought I had for Anna Macbraid, Goddess of the Mullet, was all gone. Maybe she had never been how I had thought of her. Goddess! How simple. She was just someone who wanted money and the good life more than maybe she should.

I remembered too clearly the look of her when she came running in through the door of Barratt's with her face white and crying and her shirt ripped at the shoulder. And I remembered the way she kept shaking her head when she was first questioned about who it was; and I had felt sorry for her. Then John had spoken up from the back saying

181

where was the African and somehow the blame had got laid on poor Malouf. And I remembered another thing, how John had had his head close to hers—what had he been saying to her? And the look she had then given him before she'd been hustled into the back room. What was it? Fear? Shock . . . ?

Had she been trapped into keeping quiet? Maybe. Beauty she had, but maybe not great sense either. She'd run away for the money but I wondered whether it would come to haunt her, what it was that she had done to her African guest.

I was about ready to say this when Ailish said, 'Well, I'm glad you don't, for you'd be heartbroke now that she's going and I wouldn't like you at all if you were heartbroke and mooning around like an eejit.'

'Is that so.'

She cocked her head on one side, peering at me from under her tangle of hair like a wild hedgerow bird. 'Not got too much to say for yourself, Will Cormack.'

I smiled.

'I'm off,' she said abruptly.

'What about your messages?'

'Oh yes! Here, you give them to Brede, would you; I have to hurry.' She handed me the bag and sure enough it had next to nothing in it: a loaf, a bar of soap, and tea.

She swung the bike round and started to cycle off.

'Didn't you want to go in to her yourself?'

'See you, Willie Cormack,' she called back to me. 'Make sure you're fit for the dance.'

She kind of took your breath away, Ailish King did. How was it that for all these years of seeing her day in day out, I'd not really seen her at all. I shook my head and went slowly up through the gate to Brede's.

182

Twenty

'Well,' said Brede, giving me a quizzical look, 'for a man who's a broken rib and has had his family in a fair state of panic because of his seafaring, you're walking with a fierce bounce in your step.'

'How're you, Brede?'

'I'm well.' And then with no change of expression, 'I see that young Ailish King was down to see you.'

'She had messages for you,' I said, handing over the small bag.

'Is that why she came twice, I wonder?'

'Twice?'

'I can't think what manner of a girl would bother coming to see you, Willie Cormack. The poor thing must be struck.'

I could feel my ears getting red. I hate that.

She laughed. 'I'm codding you, Willie, but she's a good girl.'

I shrugged. 'I hardly know her,' I muttered. She pulled a face which I pretended not to notice. Then a worrying thought struck me. 'Ian didn't see her, did he?'

'Ach, don't worry about him; he thinks the end of the world has struck. Are ye comin' in or what?'

I followed her into her kitchen. Not much of a cook was Brede, but then Ian never took note of what was in front of him anyhow, just shovelled it in like fuel and still stayed razor thin. Being a good cook isn't the most important of things, I reckon. She gave me a cup of tea and I asked her how Malouf was coming on.

'Him!' she smiled. 'He told me that he was a prince in his own country and that for saving him from his "distress", that was the very word he used, his "distress", he would set me up in me own palace! What would I do in a palace? The man's as odd as thirty-two left-footed boots.'

That was him all right!

'And you know,' she continued, 'he fell asleep straight after he said that, before I even had a chance to tell him he was cracked, and he hasn't woken since. He's a funny looking fella, isn't he? Maybe they're all like that in his part of Africa.'

'I wouldn't know,' I said.

'Unnatural thin, bird bones. I'm surprised he didn't break more than his arm with you two lunatics bringing him on to the beach the way you did. I'd have thought Ian would have had more sense . . . '

I didn't pay any mind to that, it was just her talking. I asked if I could see him but she wouldn't have any of it and hooshed me straight out the back of the house telling me the man needed his sleep. 'After the doctor has seen him, then you can talk to the man. Not that you'll get any sense out of him,' she sniffed. 'If he's a prince then I'm Grainne Wales.'

I told her she was the spit of the Mayo pirate.

'How dare you! She had black teeth that woman!'

'And she ate men for her breakfast?' I added.

'Mind your manners, William Cormack!'

I liked being there with her. Even with her sharp tongue and teasing ways she was easier than my own family. There wasn't anything I couldn't talk to her about except knowing how to thank her for standing against Rob Macyntire the night before, so I talked to her about the gig and the way the men of the village had been.

'Some of them,' she corrected me. She said there were always fights and drink was a curse, and she said it like it was a fact of life and meant little. I found that hard to accept, for fighting and arguing is one thing, but I remembered the way Malo had been hunted after the gig in the pub: the lads yelling and whooping, their voices thick with drink, scattered about in threes and fours.

'Rob Macyntire is a bad sort,' I said.

'He's all talk,' she said dismissively.

'I don't think so.' Macyntire didn't need drink to be dangerous. 'There aren't many who would have done what you did, Brede. None in my family, I reckon.'

She waved her hand impatiently. 'And stop looking at me like that.'

'You were soft on my dad, weren't you? Why didn't you marry him?'

'Mind your own business.' She wasn't cross though.

'Why?'

'Ach, he was a hopeless man for the ladies. He would have driven me demented with his roving. Anyway,' she said, suddenly clearing away our mugs and taking them to the sink, 'he never asked. Now out you go and talk some sense into Ian.'

'He's only worrying what we're going to do about Macyntire. That man will have the gardai on us today. I'm surprised they're not here yet.'

'You'll sort it out,' she said.

As I walked down the field with that vast Mayo sky over my head I wondered what it would be like to be in a prison, closed in, four tight walls around you and nothing but the rattle and bang of doors all day.

Ian was down working on the turf rick. I called out to him but he didn't reply, just went on mechanically, picking and placing the pieces. I found it a boring job but he always made a fine rick, one that could sit out through the worst rain and yet the turf would always be dry for burning. I sat and watched, knowing that there was little point in talking to him until he was ready.

He'd a ragged cut down his forearm that Brede had cleaned up yet it looked sore still, and a black bruise on the right side of his face. After ten minutes he came and sat beside me. 'You look fair battered,' I remarked.

'I'm all right.'

'You're lucky to have an aunt like Brede.' It wasn't the first time I'd said that to him.

He took out a crumpled pack of Sweet Aftons and, cupping his hand against the breeze, lit himself up a smoke. 'She'd drive you mad, Will,' he said, after spitting a loose strand of tobacco out the corner of his mouth like one of the old ones, 'wanting to fuss over you all the time.'

'What are we going to do, Ian?'

He squinted up at the sun as though taking his bearings at sea. 'I tell you, Willie, I'm that fed up I reckon we should disappear, right now, get on the bus and not come back.'

'We can't do that!'

'I'm not grovelling to Macyntire.'

'Malo will tell what happened.'

'We don't know what happened. He's said nothing yet. Nothing that makes any sense,' he added bitterly. 'And even if he did who'd listen to him, the crazy African who attacked Anna?'

'He never did that.'

'That's what they'll say.'

'Well, I think Robbie Macyntire's our man,' I said. 'I think he took out Malo to kill him. Him and maybe one or two others. Mrs Deane said there was more than the one in it.'

Ian finished his fag and stubbed it out on the ground. 'Do we want all this to come to law?'

'Are you serious? Of course we want the whole lot of them in front of a judge!'

He looked at me. 'I am serious. Macyntire isn't the worst of them, Willie. Have you forgotten your brother was on board too, so Mrs Deane said, and you're not going to tell me that John James was along for the ride, or as a member of the crew. Are you happy about that?'

That stopped me. I didn't like John but it was another matter having him up for attempted murder, because that's what I was thinking it was. How could the family hold up their heads with the golden boy ending up in Mountjoy? If they ever caught him, that is. Was blood thicker than water? I shook my head. 'I don't know, Ian.'

'Well, you hardly need worry, Will. No one's going to listen to us anyhow. What they'll say is that the three of us took the boat and smashed it up.' He stood up. 'I tell you, I have it figured.'

I hadn't heard him sound this bitter before, like it was lodged deep in the marrow of his bones. 'None of them will want to hear the real truth, I bet you.'

'What of Francis, Brede . . . ?' and I recalled the others standing round Brede on the beach.

'Even they will prefer some things to stay forgotten. So you can stay if you like, Willie. Malo may tell us what happened but he's just as likely to make up some fancy tale about sea monsters and drowned men. Had he been telling the truth right from the start I'd've been away off to Germany by now, you remember.' He gave a sour smile. 'Maybe I'll head for Cork instead. I can get work on the fancy yachts down there, now that I have the experience of minding one. I don't have to tell them it was only a wreck.'

'You don't think Brede will rouse the country after you?'

''Course not.'

I remembered the way she had howled out her fear on the beach the night before. 'You're wrong, Ian,' I said.

'Why don't you come with me? You'll earn a living with your fiddle. Who needs school?'

'It's not that,' I said standing up too. 'I reckon I'm not like you, Ian. I don't want to leave here.'

'Why, for God's sake? The only good thing about here is the sea and you hate that.'

I couldn't express it, not fully, not in words, not to him; but at the back of my mind I had a feeling that I would lose by leaving, lose my music. For where did the tunes come from but this, all this that was around me. Then, thinking of John James, I said, 'I don't think running is the answer either.'

A car pulled off the road and bumped down the lane towards us.

'No more than what my mother did,' he said. 'Ran into thin air.' He dusted the turf grit from his hands. 'What I would do for some money in the bank,' he sighed.

It was too late for running now for it was a garda car. Brannagh by the look of it, and a couple of others besides. I thought one of them was Francis.

'We'll be OK,' I said.

He shook his head. 'Ach, sod it, Will. I wouldn't want folk to say that Careys were always running off. We'll tell it straight so?'

'I reckon.'

I don't know what's worse: people roaring at you or them being reasonable; and listening to what you say and then not paying a blind bit of heed to it. For that is the way it was when Brannagh and Francis and the silent TJ Mulcahy, a respected fisherman who keeps his boat alongside of Francis's, came to see us.

They came in on us a bit like a posse in a western, walking with that heavy-shouldered purpose that means business. Francis in the dark glasses, talking to Brede at her doorway, and us spying on them from the field; them looking our way and Brede waving us over, and them then waiting, Francis in the middle, Brannagh a little behind and to the left, his scrubbed face looking solemn, and TJ on the right.

Has a way of looking right through you, does TJ; comes from being out at sea most of the time maybe. Eyes a bit like my dad—he's an island man too, bit younger than Dad, grizzled and wiry, his face, neck, and arms the colour of turf. A good sort but he scared the life out of us when we were just kids and liked to clamber over the boats at the pier. He never had to shout at us; we'd run at the first sight of him. I'm not sure why. I think it was because we all knew that he had a younger brother that died on him when they were out on the boats one time, and he never married, lived on his own, and was the most silent man in Blacksod.

Sure, we told them everything, starting right back with me trying to hide Malo away from the drunken crowd that were after his skin, to the moment we feared that maybe he'd been abducted. Told them it all, except that when we got to the bit about wanting to follow Macyntire's boat out to the islands I hesitated, and Ian, who was letting me do most of the talking, glanced at me and chewed his lip. Well, I didn't mention John James supposedly being on that boat. God forgive me, for I think it is wrong to hide any bit of the truth.

'You thought Rob Macyntire took the African out to the islands!' exclaimed Brannagh. 'What would he want to do that for?'

'Show him the sights,' muttered Ian. 'What do you think?'

'Mind yourself, Carey,' growled TJ.

'However he got there,' I said, 'we found Malo and he was near dead with the cold. And he wasn't fit to talk or tell us what had happened. That was it. We'd no option but to try to bring him back. Which is what we did. You'll have to ask him the rest.'

This is what Francis said: 'Maybe there was the one life in danger, and maybe not. Or maybe, as Rob and his friends are saying, the three of you went out in that curragh for a lark.' I started to interrupt. The idea was mad but he held up his hand to shut me up. 'Whatever the truth, I am not impressed. You don't take risks with the sea—you should know that, Ian. You need to think. If you had waited and asked me—'

'You were out on your boat,' said Ian.

'Amn't I back now? And there's TJ, or a couple more with decent boats who'd have gone out. Instead you took that man's boat and wrecked it and the motor. I don't mind that, bad as it is, but by rights all three of you should be dead now. Pure luck you came in and pure luck that those who came down to help you weren't drowned and all. Did you think of that?' He looked at us, the light glinting on his glasses, the breeze ruffling his hair.

I wanted to say a whole lot: that we had spent the day looking; and that somehow the village and headland seemed like a foreign land; that no one was helping; and the curragh was there; and time was precious. But I kept my mouth shut, and so did Ian. Francis and TJ, whatever about Brannagh, were practical men, they didn't have much time for the way things might have seemed to a couple of boys; facts were what they lived by.

'No one else wanted to help your man Malouf. No one,' said Ian.

'I saw him being helped last night,' said Brannaġh.

'And you saw someone, namely Robbie Macyntire, threaten to throw him back in the sea,' I countered, 'and I didn't see you shifting yourself to intervene.' It wasn't a wise thing to say to a garda, but damn me it was the truth.

Brannagh flushed and took a step forward. 'Christ! I have a good mind to box your ears, Cormack.'

And I think he would have done except TJ, who true to form had said not one word, took the wind out of his sails by saying, 'Hold it, Brannagh, the boy is right. I was there.'

'It wasn't like that,' blustered Brannagh, but when Francis glanced at him, he fell silent.

'Robbie Macyntire is not the worst,' said Francis, 'and you should be grateful that he'll not press charges, but there is a bill to pay for the making of a new boat. As for the motor, we'll go down at low tide and salvage it if we can. If you're lucky you won't have to pay for more than repair.'

'And what if Malo presses charges against Macyntire and the rest. What then?' I challenged.

'At the moment, Will, that is just wild talk and wild talk only makes matters worse.'

'But—'

'Leave it. Whatever has to be done, will be. You can count on that,' he said firmly.

'All right,' I said.

'How much is a new curragh?' Ian asked.

'It's not the money,' said TJ, 'but the time. I can make the boat, but you boys will work for me. Three months, I reckon.'

'It's a fair offer,' said Francis.

Ian looked at me and I shrugged. Of course we had to agree, for until we had any kind of proof about what really happened that night there wasn't any alternative. Mind you, I said that I wasn't that handy at making things because I am not. Dad and Gary are clever like that, but not me. I'm all thumbs, which is odd given I play the fiddle.

Behind Francis's blank shades I detected the hint of a smile, just the corner of his mouth turned down. 'Maybe TJ will have you taking his boat out, now that you have become a man of the sea like your father before you.'

'Three months' bloody work for no money,' grumbled Ian as we went back into the house.

I ignored him. 'Man of the sea?' Maybe not, but it sounded good.

Twenty-one

We tried to get Malo to press charges, but the cruel thing was, there was no proof, only Malo's word against the men who had taken him, and myself who should have been witness had been fast asleep.

And so things settled down. Ian spent his time over with TJ beginning work on the curragh we were to build and, never one to miss an opportunity, checking out the state of the *Katya*. He told me he planned to bring everything movable ashore and store it up at Blacksod—all the sails, the fittings and that. His plan was to leave just the hull, and then maybe, come next year if she survived the winter, to see what he could do to patch her up.

Meanwhile I rested at home, played my fiddle, and visited Malo, and he told me more about his village and family. And Ailish came up a few times till she became such a familiar sight that not even Ian made a fuss about it. Maybe we were all growing up. She's making me teach her some songs and she has a fine voice too though I haven't told her that yet.

Gary never went back at the end of his holidays. He had had enough, he said, of building sites in Cambridge and since there was a whole rake of new houses going up all along the Mullet, he reckoned he could do all right in the way of work here. I think that was only part of the reason he decided to stay. He belongs out here, does Gary, as maybe I do, and my father does, and others besides, and when you belong in a place perhaps it never rightly lets you go. My mother was happy, for though he is a bit of a messer and likes his late nights and his drink, he minds her and my father.

My father came home and that should have been the best thing of all. They said in the hospital that he was recovered but we all knew he was not himself really for he had lost his strength. He walked slowly with a stick and spent a lot of time up at the gable end of the house looking out to sea. Gary sometimes took him down to Barratt's for a pint but even that he found tiring.

Funny thing was that Malo would come down and sit with him, the two of them as different as sea and sky, and I heard my father giving Malo advice about how to better the sheep grazing around his village, while Malo instructed my father as to how he could get a crop of dates out here, if only he could order the sapling. 'Sure,' I heard my father say, 'there is a fine garden shop in Castlebar. They would get me a few of them trees all right.'

Of course we heard no word from John James. He never showed his face at all after Malouf's rescue. I had a feeling that maybe he and the Yank had arranged to meet up at the airport. It was fitting that them two should slide off together. His name was not mentioned in the house, nor in the village, though I know people talked

Sure, they were thieves, for I reckon something else slid off with John—that old stone with the smiling Jesus on it that the Yank had been so interested in.

You know Francis took Ian and me out to the islands a few weeks later. I think he had a notion about that Yank and John. Sure enough, the stone was gone.

'Maybe he thought he could sell it,' said Francis. 'A man like that would be all charm while he was cutting the heart out of you.'

It was hard to disagree with him.

The Sunday after we had been out to the islands Father Paul gave what for him was a powerful sermon about caring for the land, and the islands in particular, and he almost thundered against thieves and suchlike who would sell the frame off their mother's own front door if they thought there was a profit in it. And of course he talked about the Jesus stone and how it had gone and it was a sin, like selling off God.

I thought that was rich, given that it was a priest like himself who'd had the real godstone tossed into the sea. I'd probably be damned for even thinking such a thing but then one man's god is another man's devil, that's what my father used to say.

It was that Sunday too that Anna went away. There was no big send off. Indeed I wouldn't have known unless Ian and I hadn't been sitting on the wall outside the shop long after mass had finished, putting off making the long walk back to the house for our dinner, when a car rolled up. Not someone from the village at all but an Elly Bay man who sometimes acted as a taxi and he asked for the Macbraid house. We told him all right and it was Ian who asked was he taking Anna to the airport. He was a surly type and wouldn't have given her much chat on the drive.

'Will we go up and say goodbye?' said Ian.

'I don't know,' I replied. 'Maybe.'

But we didn't, I think because neither of us knew what to say to her. Funny that, after she had been the girl we had forever argued about. Now, all I knew was that she was someone I would never want to try to write a song for.

She saw us though, and made her taxi stop. Oh, it was all as if nothing had happened, almost. She got out and gave us each a hug, and talked in that hurried way she had when she was excited. She told us that this had happened all of a sudden or else she would have done the rounds and said goodbye, and God, she was unhappy to be missing the curragh race but we must be sure to write to her, her mam had the address, and tell how we did and she would surely be home the following summer . . .

194

And then she was away, a hand waving from the open window. I didn't think we would see her again either.

August was fine and my rib healed up all right and although we didn't win the curragh race, we gave the winners a good run and if Ian and I are still talking next summer we may well beat them. It was a great day, the little strand at Blacksod packed with people, and all the boats and bustle of crews getting ready and shouting out to each other, and some that had not practised or had been up too late the night before failing fast, or cracking into each other like eejits. Gary brought Brede, Malo, and my mother and father down, and gave me such a slap on the back when we came ashore that I thought he'd bust my mended rib all over again.

And of course Ailish was there. She was bouncing up and down when we pulled into the slipway after the race, shouting her head off, and then just as we came alongside she jumped into the curragh and gave me a kiss. I felt a right idiot trying to ship the oar and keep me balance and the crowd all watching. But she's like that, doesn't give a damn. She gave a whoop and leapt right into the water splashing us both, in her clothes and all. Ian grinned at me. 'Sure you don't want to escape while you have the chance?' he said.

That was maybe the high point of the summer for that night was the big do in Barratt's and I played a couple of sets with some of the old fellas, and there was great dancing and everybody was remarking how Ailish was mighty changed in herself and not at all the tomboy she'd once been. She danced to one of the sets I played and I swear that her hair was flame and her heels were fire, she was that good. And that night I walked her home and she kissed me softly, and not for show or for the excitement, and it somehow washed away much of the bad things that had happened.

195

'I wonder,' she said, 'in one year's time where we'll be?'

I shrugged. 'I'm not going anywhere,' I said. But I thought she looked sad, as if she knew something I did not.

'Is that right?' she said, and she went in and shut the door quietly behind her and I had a long walk home and without even Ian to keep me company.

Malo wouldn't come to the dance. As he recovered he grew more and more quiet and drawn in on himself and when he wasn't sitting with my father, one or other of them sleeping more often than not, he was walking the shore, picking up bits of wood or things washed up, bottles, broken dolls, things of no value at all. And you know what he told me? 'I am looking for the way home.'

I think he really did go odd in his head. One time he went into the church and drank a whole bottle of the altar wine. The priest went mad, and so did half the parish. Malo didn't care. He said he was thirsty and it was bad drink anyhow and why wouldn't the priest give the people good water to drink instead. I thought it a laugh—and I reckon he had a point too.

Brede tried to keep an eye on him as much as she could and there was some talk of raising money to get him an air fare home, but that never came to anything. I think perhaps because everyone wanted to forget about the business when Malo had been hunted like a dog, and maybe he didn't help himself. I don't know. I don't blame him for anything.

He was in a fight one night, in Barratt's. He went right up to Macyntire and knocked the pint he was drinking out of his hand, told him he was a 'cur', so Gary reported, and threw a punch smack in the middle of his face. Macyntire was so surprised he fell back over his chair: 'Legs up in the air like a fat clown. It was great!' said Gary.

He didn't say how he had had to restrain Rob Macyntire from coming after Malo with a busted bottle, and had to promise that Malo would never go drinking there again. But of course Malouf didn't go there to drink anyhow. I now know what he was doing, he was settling his score, preparing to leave, not run away, just leave.

I was up with Ian at TJ's, just the fetcher, while the two of them worked and talked. Ian was good, could shape and bend and had a feel for the work. TJ said he could make his living as a builder of curraghs if there was the demand, which there might be round and about the place. We were doing well and it was certainly going to take a lot less than the three months we'd anticipated, but we were busy and Ian had no time to do the clearing work he had wanted to do on *Katya*. It didn't seem that urgent anyhow, for after the initial interest everyone left the wreck well alone. Until, that is, a fine yacht came sailing into the bay, and moored right there in Elly.

A Dublin two-master she was, towing a big dinghy behind her. We stopped work to watch her sail by. 'Longboat,' TJ said, referring to the dinghy. 'I heard some fella sailed all the way to Australia in one. Mad.'

Funnily enough we saw young people from the yacht sailing the longboat that evening. They came up the coast to us at Blacksod pier, moored and came in for a drink; must have been in their twenties I suppose, three of them.

When I told Malo he perked right up and insisted we all go down to see the yacht. So we did. We took our bikes and cycled and sat on the shore watching them—apart from the ones who had sailed the dinghy there were at least four more on board. They must have had money for she was a fine big yacht and she gleamed.

They seemed mighty interested in the *Katya*, for they motored over to it at high tide, circling it again and again. They went to and fro a couple of times, and even climbed aboard and had a look around. Ian was for yelling at them but for some reason Malo restrained him. 'No,' he said in that simple way of his, 'they can look. Why not.'

The next day Malo came down to the pier at Blacksod; it wasn't like him at all but I took it as a good sign that he was getting back to normal. He watched us work, asked TJ about this and that and about the longboat sailing dinghy. He seemed interested in that all right, and when they sailed it up to the pier again, he strolled down to have a look at it.

He was quiet in himself that night, I remember. Brede said he tucked into a good meal and went to bed early.

The next morning Malouf was gone.

The man was cracked after all. And he never said goodbye. I found that hard, we all did. And he left a fine stir behind him too for not only was he gone but that big Dublin family were roaring and yelling and accusing everyone left, right, and centre that someone had stolen their longboat. Francis had to deal with them, and of course he and we knew what had happened.

'Is that madman trying to sail home?' he asked me.

'He is surely.'

There was a search: Francis and TJ took out their boats, they radioed down the coast, they even got the helicopter out from Shannon to scour for him, but there was no sign.

'I don't reckon he made it round Achill head,' said Francis. 'A small boat like that, caught by a squall, could have shipped water and gone, just like that.'

Still, the search went on. It was even on local radio. Three days they searched and then very quietly, it ended. All hope, they reckoned, was gone.

Now you would have thought I'd have been sad, and I was; but the strange thing is, when there's no body there's no real death either. I can't explain it properly but though I was sad, sort of empty, I wasn't as sad as I felt I should have been. This man who had in a funny way shaken all our lives

198

had just gone away, much as Anna had, and John James, and the Yank too.

The Dubliners left, roaring and threatening, and it then turned out they weren't a nice bunch at all. Ian went down to *Katya* the morning after they sailed, and there wasn't a fitting or item of value that they hadn't stripped from that wreck. 'She's nothing but busted concrete now,' he said bitterly. 'No future in her at all.'

And so the summer went away too.

We finished the boat and Rob Macyntire, curse him, received it with a nod. His engine was fixed too, and I didn't like giving him either, but despite all the wrongs of it he had the law on his side, so we did what we had to.

With the end of August school started, at least for me and Ailish. Ian had a blazing row with Brede and then with our form teacher, and he walked out. School was never for him anyhow.

He came to say goodbye and we walked nearly the whole of the headland together. He's going to make his way to Cork and find work; maybe to England for a while, in a couple of years when he's seventeen or so. He said he'd be back. I hope so. Before he went he gave me an old leather folder that he wanted me to mind for him. It was his deed to land on the island. John James had never come up with the money—and now, he said, he was glad. He said if anything happened I was to have it. I told him he was an idiot and we shook hands.

I think his going broke Brede's heart, though she smiled about it and said you could never expect someone like Ian to stay in a place like this, for he had that much of his mother in him.

With Ian gone and Malouf lost, it was maybe no surprise that in the late autumn storms that we had that year *Katya* slowly started to break up till there was hardly anything that you'd recognize of a boat left about her.

Mrs Macbraid heard from Anna all right, all set up with a job and all, and leading the fine life. But there was never a mention of John James or the Yank, bad luck to them. And we never heard a whisper of the smiling Jesus. Probably sitting in some man's garage I reckon.

And that seemed to be the end of it all, except that Ian turned up again for a few days at Christmas. He'd found work down in Cork and was doing OK. I remember I played at Barratt's. I played two songs that night, on my own. I hadn't felt like playing them before, I don't know why. One was for Gary, a great rough jig that had the place stamping and clapping, and my brother actually wept, can you believe it? What a soft heart he has after all, and he pestered me for days till he had the tune of it fixed in his head.

The second was the tune that had haunted me all summer, slowly coming at me, bit by bit—until I just about had it right. It was different from anything I'd ever played in public before, longer than most tunes and not one you could dance to, but the place fell quiet as they listened. It had its ending, sad and long was the way of it, so it kind of floated off.

Ailish asked why I played it then when we were all so happy. I said it was for Malo and his going.

She said, 'If I go, will you write something like that for me?'

I didn't give her a straight answer because I felt I would never write anything like that again.

We never found the godstone, though Francis and I talked about it a fair bit and he took me and Ailish out to the Inishkeas plenty of times the following summer and I showed him where Ian had dived and how Malo had heard the voices of all the men of the island who had drowned in that storm. Francis said a wise thing: 'Why look for the stone, Willie, if it is there all the time?'

My father missed Malouf and refused to believe he was dead. 'That man,' he said, 'was a cut above other men. I'd say he will become president of his country one day. Something like that.'

My father, I think, had extravagant expectations, which was why I was reluctant to tell him we'd never found the godstone. Eventually I did and to my surprise he didn't seem to mind at all.

'Francis is maybe right,' he said. 'Under water, or over water, if it is there, what does it matter. And I think it must be there, because you know your African friend,' which was always how he referred to Malo, 'actually heard my father talking to him that time he should have drowned. And I would say that was the work of the godstone. A great miracle that, Willie.'

He had both hands leaning on his walking stick and he was in his favourite spot in the lee of the house, looking out to the south island, remembering maybe the little white house on the shore of the harbour, and his mother and his brothers and sisters, now all gone.

'Yes, Dad,' I said.

'And you have lost that fear you had?'

'I have.'

'That is a great thing too.' The wind and bright light made his eyes water and he'd wipe them from time to time with the cuff of his shirt, but they were still as blue as the sky. 'And you never heard from that African friend of yours?'

'No.'

'Well,' he said, turning to make his way back into the house, 'never give up hope for I think all things come round in the end.'

Perhaps they do, for later that summer a scrubby postcard with an Algerian stamp landed through the door.

'My good thief,' the message read, 'I am home. Do you remember what I said to you one time? You cannot drown in the desert. Come to Ideles. M.'

Other Oxford children's novels

The Scavenger's Tale   Rachel Anderson
ISBN 0 19 271736 7

The taller Monitor placed her hand on my shoulder.

   'You can't,' I squealed. 'My family's opted out.'

   'Nobody opts out, pet. Every human being has the potential to offer the gift of life to another. Now take it easy. Just a little shot. A nice sedative.'
She took the sterile wrapping off a syringe-pak while the other held me . . .

It is 2015, after the great Conflagration, and London has become a tourist sight for people from all over the world, coming to visit the historic Heritage Centres. These are out of bounds to people like Bedford and his sister Dee who live in an Unapproved Temporary Dwelling and have to scavenge from skips and bins just to stay alive.

Bedford begins to notice something odd about the tourists: when they arrive in the city, they are desperately ill, but when they leave they seem to have been miraculously cured. And then the Dysfuncs start disappearing. It is only when a stranger appears, terribly injured, that Bedford begins to put two and two together . . .

Shadows   Tim Bowler

ISBN 0 19 271802 9

Jamie stared into his father's eyes and saw only a dark unyielding obsession.

Jamie knows what to expect if he doesn't win: Jamie's father is obsessed with the idea that Jamie will become a world squash champion, that Jamie will succeed where he had not. But Jamie doesn't share his father's single-minded ambition and is desperate to escape from the verbal and physical abuse that will follow when he fails.

Then Jamie finds the girl hiding in his shed, and in helping her to escape from her past and the danger that is pursuing her Jamie is able to put his own problems into perspective. He realizes that he can't run away for ever—he must come out of the shadows and face up to his father, however painful the process might be.

River Boy   Tim Bowler

ISBN 0 19 271756 1
Also in mass-market paperback ISBN 0 19 275035 6
Winner of the Carnegie Medal

Standing at the top of the fall, framed against the sky, was the figure of a boy. At least, it looked like a boy, though he was quite tall and it was hard to make out his features against the glare of the sun. She watched and waited, uncertain what to do, and whether she had been seen.

When Jess's grandfather has a serious heart attack, surely their planned trip to his boyhood home will have to be cancelled? But Grandpa insists on going so that he can finish his final painting, 'River Boy'. As Jess helps her ailing grandfather with his work, she becomes entranced by the scene he is painting. And then she becomes aware of a strange presence in the river, the figure of a boy, asking her for help and issuing a challenge that will stretch her swimming talents to the limits. But can she take up the challenge before it is too late for Grandpa . . . and the River Boy?

Tightrope   Gillian Cross

ISBN 0 19 271804 5 (hardback)   ISBN 0 19 271750 2 (paperback)

'There's someone of mine in every street round here. In every pub and every block of flats. I'm the ringmaster and they all jump when I crack the whip.'

Eddie Beale looks after his friends, people say, as long as they entertain him. And when he takes notice of Ashley, she is happy to put on a show and be part of the excitement that surrounds him and his gang—it is a relief from the unrelenting drudgery of her life. Then she realizes that someone else is also watching her. Someone is stalking her and leaving messages that get uglier and uglier. Can Eddie help her? And if he does, what price will she have to pay?

Pictures in the Dark   Gillian Cross

ISBN 0 19 271741 3

Something struck across the pool of light, swimming fast. The smooth orange surface was fractured by a strong, V-shaped pattern of ripples. It was too late to stop his finger. It was already pressing the shutter release, to take the photograph.

When Charlie takes the photograph of the unknown animal swimming in the river that night, he has no idea of the effect it will have on his life and the weird events it will set in motion.

Why is Peter, the boy with the strange, staring eyes, so obsessed by the picture? And what is it about Peter that upsets everybody so much—even his own father?

When Charlie tries to help Peter and protect him from the bullying, he is led deeper into the secret, mysterious life of the river bank, and the creatures that inhabit it.

Humanzee   Susan Gates

ISBN 0 19 271796 0

'He's just an animal, isn't he? Anyone with any brains can see that. But he walks upright and he looks a bit human, that's all. So I call him humanzee, half-man, half-chimpanzee, see.'

'You can't put people in cages,' said Nemo, appalled. So he persuades his parents to buy Chingwe, the humanzee, and take him with them as they tour the country with their travelling Flea Circus. But it is not so easy to cope with an old and emotionally upset humanzee, especially when the scientists want to experiment on him, and other people object to his very existence and come after him with guns. Nemo has to think fast to save Chingwe from the dangers that are threatening him.

Iron Heads   Susan Gates

ISBN 0 19 271755 3

'No! Don't go into the fog! You'll never find your way out!'

When Rachel's parents get jobs on an offshore island, her main worry is when the wind turbine will be installed so that she can play her CDs. But then she notices some weird things happening. Her brother, Stevie, always untidy, insists that everything in his room should be in straight lines, facing the same way. The island rabbits dig their burrows in parallel lines, facing north. Why don't the Islanders get lost in the fog? And why did the last warden's house burn down? As she tries to find the answers to these mysteries, Rachel has to act quickly to prevent another tragedy.

207

Atlantis   Frances Mary Hendry
ISBN 0 19 271751 0

A creak, a crunching growl, a roar. A brief dazzle of light. He tried to leap for the wall, as the Coal had told him to do, but his bad ankle gave way.
  The roof fell in.

In rocky caverns deep below the Antarctic ice lies the new kingdom of Atlantis. The Atlantans have lived there for centuries, safe from the cold and darkness Outside and watched over by their Gods. Until one day, a boy called Mungith decides to take his trial for Adulthood by working in the old coal mines, shoring up the crumbling roofs. What he discovers there puts the whole of Atlantis in danger and could bring their ordered and peaceful existence to an end.

Atlantis in Peril   Frances Mary Hendry
ISBN 0 19 271789 8

She had to get away. She had to go outside, to find the Giants.

The Giant had brought disaster on the City and the good name of Chooker's family was tarnished. Chooker decides that the only way to restore the people's faith in her House, and in Mungith, her cousin, who found the Giant in the Mines, is to go Outside, find the other Giants, and prove that they are not all bad. And when Hemminal, the ex-Wilder and sister of the King, tries to kill Chooker in order to stop her, it only makes Chooker realize how urgent her mission is . . .

Plundering Paradise   Geraldine McCaughrean

ISBN 0 19 271547 X

Nathan felt his stomach cramp and his heart fill up. Go among the pirates?
See pirates, in their natural habitat? They were the stuff of all his
daydreams; they were the very people he had thought about all his dull
childhood—the beacons that had lit his way through every bleak, grey
day of his bleak, grey life. But did he want to meet any? Did he really want
to see the genuine item?

Nathan's daydreams about pirates come to an abrupt end when he
is summoned to see the headmaster of his school, only to be told
that two terms' fees have not been paid and he must leave the
school immediately.

When Tamo White—the son of a pirate—suggests that Nathan
go home with him to Madagascar, it seems to Nathan as if his
daydreams might come true—but then he remembers his sister,
Maud. How could he take 'Mousy Maud' to a strange land,
peopled by savages and home to cut-throats and pirates? But Maud
seems to like the idea . . .

Stones in Water   Donna Jo Napoli

ISBN 0 19 271798 7

'You have to fight. I don't mean with your fists. I mean inside. Don't ever let them win over the inside of you.'

Roberto and his friend Samuele are rounded up by German soldiers and put on a train. They are now part of the war, providing forced labour at various work camps deep inside Nazi territory. Their new life is unbearable—backbreaking work, near starvation, and, through it all, desperately keeping Samuele's secret—a secret that, if discovered, would mean death for them both.

Escape becomes Roberto's only chance, but can he survive the brutal winter cold, with only the gift stone from the Jewish girl in the camp to give him hope that he will ever see his home again?

Sweet Clarinet   James Riordan

ISBN 0 19 271795 2

I would gladly have welcomed death with a passion—as long as it stopped the pain. 'Oh, God, let me die, please, please, let me die. I'll say my prayers every night, honest, if only you let me die.'

Billy thought growing up in wartime was fun: the fiery skies, exploding factories, the noise of the blitz, playing among the rubble of the bombed houses. But then a bomb fell directly on the shelter where Billy and his mother had gone to escape the bombardment and changed Billy's life for ever.

Billy wakes up in hospital, horribly burned and longing for death—angry at a world in which he will always be a freak, an object of horror or pity, an outcast—until a precious gift from a soldier who is also disfigured gives him hope and a reason for living.

Starlight City   Sue Welford

ISBN 0 19 271791 X

'Where?' I asked. 'Where will you go?'

'The City,' she said.

'The City! Have you got any idea what it's like there? You won't last five minutes.'

It is the year 2050. When Kari's mother brings home a weird old woman she finds wandering in the road, Kari is appalled. What could have possessed her mother to pick up a scruffy old Misfit— or even a Drifter?

But Kari soon realizes there is more to Rachel than she first thought. There is something about her—her soft voice, her gentle aura, her love of music—which wins Kari over. So when the police arrive, looking for Rachel, and take her away for questioning, Kari decides she must go to the City and look for her, not realizing that this is just the beginning of an adventure that will change her life . . .